Georgia leaned in to Ivy. 'Looks like your
sister has herself a royal admirer!'
The realisation hit Ivy like a stake in the gut.
Alex likes Olivia! A second thought followed
almost as quickly. *But Olivia has a boyfriend.*

Sink your fangs into these:

MY SISTER THE VAMPIRE

Switched

Fangtastic!

Revamped!

Vampalicious

Take Two

Love Bites

Lucky Break

Star Style

Twin Spins!

Date with Destiny

Flying Solo

Stake Out!

Double Disaster!

Flipping Out!

Secrets and Spies

Fashion Frightmare

MY BROTHER THE WEREWOLF

Cry Wolf!

Puppy Love!

Howl-oween!

Tail Spin

Sienna Mercer

MY SISTER THE VAMPIRE

LOVE BITES

EGMONT

With special thanks to Sara O'Connor

For Sara G. Because I knew you . . .

EGMONT
We bring stories to life

My Sister the Vampire: Love Bites first published in Great Britain 2011
by Egmont UK Limited
The Yellow Building, 1 Nicholas Road, London W11 4AN

Copyright © Working Partners Ltd 2011
Created by Working Partners Limited, London WC1X 9HH

ISBN 978 1 4052 5698 8

7 9 10 8

www.egmont.co.uk

A CIP catalogue record for this title is available from the British Library

Typeset by Avon DataSet Ltd, Bidford on Avon, Warwickshire
Printed and bound in Great Britain by the CPI Group

47583/9

MIX
Paper
FSC FSC® C018306

EGMONT LUCKY COIN

Our story began over a century ago, when seventeen-year-old
Egmont Harald Petersen found a coin in the street.

He was on his way to buy a flyswatter, a small hand-operated
printing machine that he then set up in his tiny apartment.

The coin brought him such good luck that today Egmont has
offices in over 30 countries around the world. And that lucky
coin is still kept at the company's head offices in Denmark.

Chapter One

'I promise I'll be quick,' Olivia Abbott told her sister. She kicked the snow off her fuzzy wool boots outside the east entrance to the Franklin Grove mall.

'As long as I don't have to spend my morning surrounded by crazy, screaming fan girls,' Ivy replied. The doors slid open and blasted hot air in their faces, sending Ivy's black hair and matching scarf flitting behind her.

As they walked inside the mall past all the familiar stores, Olivia said, 'We're more than an hour early. How busy can a book signing be?'

She checked her reflection in the window of Trudy's Beauty Palace. She was wearing her favourite jeans, pink-and-white striped sweater and rhinestone belt. It had been over a week since she'd last seen her movie-star boyfriend, Jackson, and it would be at least another week before she got to see him again – so she wanted to look her best.

Since the film set of *The Groves* had left town a few weeks before, Jackson had called her every day and visited at weekends whenever he could. It was hard dating from a distance, and it was going to be even harder tomorrow when Olivia and Ivy left for Transylvania for a week's vacation.

Olivia picked up a noise, a hum of voices that got louder with each step. The twins turned a corner and Olivia couldn't believe her eyes. They stopped at exactly the same moment, shocked by the roped-off line of girls that wove across most of the huge atrium in the centre of the mall. The bookstore wasn't even open yet, but it looked like an entire prom was waiting outside.

Ivy looked at the huge line. 'Tell me this line is for free ice cream day.'

Olivia crinkled her nose. 'I don't think so.'

One girl at the front was clutching the entire set of Action Jackson dolls, and the girl behind her had a photo of Jackson on her T-shirt. The next girl was dressed up as an ice skater, the love interest in Jackson's first movie, and the girl after that was holding the Caulfield Collection DVD box set of Jackson's first six movies which, Olivia knew from personal experience, was very hard to get hold of. These girls weren't waiting for a chocolate-dipped cone; they were waiting to gawk and giggle at and get autographs from *Olivia's* boyfriend. It made her feel like a wet pom pom.

'Revenge of the glitter zombie hoard,' Ivy

said, flinging her hands up like a cheesy horror movie actress.

'It's fine,' Olivia said, pulling out her cell phone. 'I'll call him and we'll say a quick hello before the doors open.'

She dialled Jackson's number but it went straight to his voicemail.

'Um.' Olivia hadn't prepared for this. She had told him last night that she was going to come to see him before the signing. *Why hasn't he left his phone on?* She took a deep breath. 'No big deal. I'm sure Jackson's told the security guard to expect us.'

Olivia led her twin past the crowd towards the front of the line.

'The glitter zombies are looking at us,' Ivy whispered, pulling on Olivia's sweater, still pretending to be afraid.

'Don't make eye contact.' Olivia plastered her sweetest smile on her face and kept going. But she could feel four hundred eyes watching her every step.

They reached the store entrance. The windows were covered with pictures of Jackson and pink and red hearts.

'Be Jackson Caulfield's Valentine,' the sign boasted. 'Buy his book and get it autographed!'

But I'm *his Valentine!* Olivia thought.

A security guard with an earpiece stood in front of the door with his arms crossed.

'Good morning, sir,' Olivia said, knowing that a little politeness could go a long way. But, like a secret-service man at the White House, he didn't even flinch.

Olivia refused to give up easily. She took a step forwards and put her hand on the door.

The security guard thrust his arm across the door, right in front of her face. 'Where do you think you're going?'

'I'm here to see Jackson,' Olivia replied.

'Yeah, you and every other girl in this line.' He didn't move his arm.

She didn't want to have to do it, but she didn't have a choice. 'Really, you should let me in.' She leaned closer. 'I'm Jackson's girlfriend.'

'You can't be!' shouted the girl with the action figures. '*I'm* his girlfriend.'

'You are *not*.' The ice-skating girl looked ready to spit sequins. 'I am!'

'Don't be ridiculous,' put in the girl with the photo T-shirt. 'Last month, he autographed my magazine "Love, Jackson".' She thrust a crumpled magazine under the other girls' noses. 'See? I've got *proof*!'

Olivia felt like she'd tripped flat on her face during a cheer. She didn't know what to say.

Ivy leaned in and said to the security guard, 'Look, Jackson really is expecting to see us today.

Can't you . . . uh . . . check your list?'

'There's no list, young lady. Just that line behind you, filled with two hundred of Jackson's "girlfriends".' He pointed to the end of the line, which had doubled in size since they'd arrived. 'Everyone has to wait their turn.'

'You'd *better* not be trying to cut in line,' said the girl with the action figures.

Ice-skater Girl glared at them. 'We've been waiting here for *hours*! Who do you think you are?'

'Uh, I, um –' Olivia didn't know what to say. If she told them that she really *was* Jackson's girlfriend, she could get lynched. *I must be the only girl in the world who has to* line up *to see her own boyfriend*, Olivia thought.

'No, no,' Ivy told the girls. 'We're not cutting. Not at all. Excuse us, please!' Ivy pulled Olivia away from the line. 'Did you see the look in their eyes, Olivia? I may be a vampire,' Ivy muttered, 'but these girls scare me.'

'Olivia, darling!' called a familiar voice.

She looked back to see Charlotte Brown, the captain of the cheerleaders, waving her over. Olivia felt her already twisted stomach do another flip. Olivia spent lots of time with Charlotte on the squad and knew that Charlotte was mean even when she was trying to be nice.

'You're not in line yet? Did you sleep through your alarm?' Charlotte asked sweetly. Her blonde hair was messy and her frilly silk blouse looked crumpled.

She couldn't have, Olivia thought. *She wouldn't. Did Charlotte —*

'Did you camp out overnight?' demanded Ivy.

'Of course not!' Charlotte smirked. 'Katie did it for me. I've only been here for three hours.' She teased her hair with her fingers. 'But I'm going for the "camped out overnight"

8

look for the TV cameras.'

Olivia couldn't believe even Charlotte was willing to wait hours.

'Too bad you can't use your "special friendship" with Jackson to skip the line,' Charlotte went on, using the biggest air-quotes Olivia had ever seen when she said 'special friendship'. 'You know, this *could* look to some people like you might have, um . . . *stretched the truth* about being his girlfriend.'

Olivia's jaw dropped. *She did* not *just say that!* But she kept quiet – she didn't want to get kicked off the squad.

Ivy stepped in. 'And *this* could look like you were paying someone to be your Valentine.'

Charlotte narrowed her eyes. 'Paying is clearly something you have a problem with, freak, judging from all those second-hand clothes.'

'This is *vintage!*' Ivy retorted, smoothing down her black satin high-waisted skirt.

This is so not *how I pictured my morning,* Olivia thought. 'Ivy, let's go to the back of the line before it's out of the building.'

She stomped to the end of the line, her face blushing, and crossed her arms.

'Yeah, back where you belong,' taunted one of the girls.

'Just ignore her,' whispered Ivy. 'She's wearing a pink glittery scrunchie.'

Olivia gazed down the long line of girls holding signs with her boyfriend's picture on them. Twenty different Jacksons were watching from the posters plastered around the atrium. His face was everywhere – but Olivia had never felt so far from her boyfriend.

❤   🦇   🦇

'I can't take any more of this torture,' Ivy whispered.

Ivy Vega decided she could ignore the pink streamers hanging from the ceiling, and she

10

was pretending not to notice the cut-out hearts covering every store window. But being stuck in line listening to love-struck girls randomly bursting into romantic songs from Jackson's movies was just too much.

'I'm so sorry,' Olivia mumbled for, probably, the thirty-seventh time.

Ivy gave her sister another hug.

'It's not the waiting that's annoying; it's the *Valentine's*.' Ivy just hoped she could escape soon. No matter how much they tried to sell it to her, she couldn't buy into the whole stupid cupids-and-candy-hearts scene. In two days from now, couples around the world would be exchanging cards because stationery companies had told them to. She just didn't get the commercial side of romance.

There was a young girl in front of them, with brown ringlets framing her face and a cute

11

red denim jacket. She turned around and said, 'Hi, I'm Janie!' Then she a thrust a little box out towards the twins. 'Candy heart?'

'Oh no, I'm melting . . .' Ivy pretended to crumple to her knees.

Janie looked at Ivy like she really was melting.

Olivia intervened, taking a candy that was the same shade of pink as her lip gloss. 'Thanks so much,' she said to Janie and then whispered to Ivy, 'Don't be such a V-day humbug!'

Ivy thought conversation candy hearts were pure evil, but she took one to be polite.

'Mine says, "Kiss me".' Olivia popped it in her mouth.

'Well, this one says, "Sweetheart",' said Ivy, holding the offensive object like it was a clove of garlic.

'Aren't you going to eat it?' Janie asked.

Ivy forced a smile and bit into the chewy,

dry candy. She grinned wickedly at her sister. 'I wonder where the expression "sweetheart" came from. Actual hearts? I'm sure mine would be more of a *sour* heart.'

'Ew!' Olivia crinkled her nose and Ivy chuckled.

Ivy's vegetarian twin got squeamish at the mere suggestion of blood. *Good thing she's the bunny, and I'm the vampire*, Ivy thought.

Ivy and Olivia were twins born to a vampire father and a human mother and had only met each other at the beginning of the school year. Olivia's adoptive parents had moved to Franklin Grove and the sisters had been getting to know each other, and all about their biological family background, ever since.

Olivia nudged her sister. 'Has Brendan given you any candy hearts for Valentine's?' she asked.

Ivy felt her face form a scowl. 'He knows I can't stand all this cheesy Valentine's stuff.'

Olivia pretended to gasp. 'No pressies?'

Ivy did like presents, but she wasn't interested in teddy bears with 'I WUV YOU' written on their tummies. 'I don't need material possessions to reinforce the strength of our relationship,' Ivy declared.

'But Valentine's presents are the best,' Olivia replied. 'It's my ultimate favourite holiday. I can't wait to see what . . . you know who . . . will get me.'

'Jackson's going to be my Valentine,' Janie boasted. 'I've saved this one just for him.' She opened up her hand to show a candy heart that read 'I HEART YOU'.

Despite the message's assault on grammar, even Ivy thought it was sweet.

'Jackson Caulfield is the dreamiest dream!' declared Janie.

Olivia smiled. 'He is pretty nice.'

The little girl squealed. 'Ohmigosh, have you met him?'

Olivia started to explain. 'Well, a few weeks ago when that film crew was in town . . .'

Ivy's mind floated back to Brendan. She wondered if he was playing video games or practising tricks on his new dirt bike. Maybe she could call him to help her through the eternity of waiting in this line?

As Olivia chatted with Janie, Ivy rummaged in her big black messenger bag for her phone.

'Ohmigosh, you're in a movie with him!' Janie gushed. 'You're like a film star!'

'No, no,' Olivia replied. 'It was just a small part.'

Ivy finally found her phone sandwiched between her notebook and a vinyl record of The Killer Bees.

But as she started to dial his number, she caught sight of a black-clad figure with curly black hair striding across the lobby. Her pulse raced – it was Brendan.

What is he doing in the mall? By himself? Ivy thought. The third Dark Violet album wasn't available until next week and he'd already bought the new sarcophagus racing game. They'd had a tournament yesterday which Ivy had won. What else could he possibly want to buy?

Still clutching her phone, she watched him stop and look in the window of Hannah's Homewares. He went inside but came out a few moments later empty-handed, with a determined set to his jaw. He glanced at a stationery shop, festooned in red ribbons. *Could he . . .* Ivy started to think, *be shopping for Valentine's?*

'Ha!' Ivy laughed out loud.

'What?' Olivia asked.

'Brendan,' Ivy hissed.

'In line for Jackson's autograph?' Olivia

looked around, incredulous.

'No, over there.' Ivy pointed him out. He was peering in the window of the luggage store at a row of big leather purses.

Olivia giggled. 'Looks like he's after some material possessions to buy for you.'

'He couldn't be,' Ivy replied. He knew she thought Valentine's Day was just a made-up holiday to trick bunnies into buying mass-produced emotion.

'OK, if he isn't buying you a Valentine's gift,' Olivia said, 'why is he staring at ladies' luggage accessories?'

Brendan had crouched down by a display of matching green key chains, wallets and bag tags with a big sign that said 'Leather Madness!'

Ivy pushed the call button on her phone and watched Brendan jump. He fumbled with his jacket pocket, pulled out his phone and tentatively put it to his ear.

'Hey, Ivy,' he said and she could hear the weirdness in his voice. Ivy watched him stop and lean against a wall. He couldn't see her but she could see him.

'Hey,' she replied. 'Whatcha doing?'

'Not much.' Brendan ran his hand through his hair. 'Just hanging out at the Meat and Greet, waiting for you.'

Ivy narrowed her eyes. Something was definitely going on. 'But we're not supposed to be meeting there for another two hours.'

'Uh, yeah.' He pushed himself off the wall and started pacing. 'Since you're leaving tonight, I don't want to miss a single minute of our goodbye lunch.'

At the mention of 'goodbye', Ivy felt the bats fluttering in her tummy for the thousandth time. A few weeks ago, she and Olivia had done everything they could think of to find out about their real parents. It took a lot of work and a little luck but they finally discovered that the dad Ivy had grown up with, the dad she thought was her adoptive vampire father, was actually their real father. And, to top it all off, he was the son of a Transylvanian Count. To him, it was no big deal, but to Ivy and Olivia it was unbelievable. Suddenly, they were vampire royalty!

After much pestering, he had agreed to write to his parents with the whole Ivy and Olivia story, even though he hadn't spoken to them in years. 'If it will make you happy,' their dad had said.

'I know you have to go,' Brendan said quietly into the phone now, 'but I'm really going to miss you.'

'I'll miss you, too,' Ivy replied. It would be the only time they'd been apart since he'd asked her out on their first date to the mall. But it would be worth it. She really wanted to know what her grandparents – the Count and Countess – were like.

Ivy had memorised the letter her grandmother had sent back:

Dear Karl,

Your father and I would be so grateful to meet our granddaughters and welcome them into the family. Let us ignore the past. We enclose three first-class tickets leaving next month, in the hope that you will visit us.

Love,

Mother

Ivy instinctively reached for the ring that she wore around her neck; Olivia had an identical one. Matching emerald rings with their family symbol – the outline of an eye with a V in the middle – engraved inside. After a lifetime of not knowing, she was finally going to find out where she came from.

This week in Europe was going to be killer, but first she had to figure out what her boyfriend was up to.

'So what's the burger special today?' Ivy asked innocently, seeing how far he would go to conceal where he was. Olivia covered her mouth to stifle a giggle.

'It's, uh . . .' Brendan looked around frantically. 'Green leather madness,' he blurted.

Ivy snorted. 'That doesn't sound very appetising.'

'Well, I'm not going to order one,' he replied.

'It doesn't *sound* like you're at the Meat and Greet,' Ivy tried again. 'I can't hear any music in the background.'

'I think they've turned it off for a minute,' Brendan replied, talking faster and faster.

Ivy decided to let him off the hook. He wasn't going to confess. 'OK, well, I'll see you at noon,' she said.

'OK, bye,' he almost shouted and Ivy watched him collapse against the wall.

'He would *not* keep it a secret if he wasn't shopping for you,' Olivia pointed out.

Ivy saw him stride away. 'I'm going after him,' she declared.

'I'll be here,' Olivia said, looking morosely at the line in front of her.

'With me!' said Janie. 'Another candy heart?'

Ivy darted across the lobby after Brendan, pressing herself against the walls. She followed him at a safe distance down the east wing of the mall. She had to be extra careful; Brendan was a vampire, after all, and might be able to sense her if she got too close.

What do spies in movies do? Ivy thought. *Melt into*

the crowd. She looked down at her black skirt and heavy boots. *Well, that's not gonna happen.* She'd just have to be . . . discreet.

Brendan went into Trudy's Beauty Palace and Ivy ducked in and hid behind a rack of shampoo bottles. She peered between two mannequin heads displaying blonde wigs to see Brendan browsing the accessories in the glass counter. There were sparkly bracelets, dangly earrings, rings and brooches – nothing that her gorgeous goth boyfriend would ever buy for himself.

Oh my darkness! Ivy thought. *He* must *be shopping for Valentine's.*

Brendan turned around and Ivy ducked behind the hair pieces, just in time.

If he's buying me *something, I have to buy* him *something,* Ivy realised. *A present that is as good as whatever he gets me.* As Brendan left the store empty-handed, Ivy decided she had to follow him until she saw what he bought.

She crept along behind him, staying out of sight.

Be like water, Ivy told herself. Olivia's martial-arts-obsessed dad had taught her that. She slid from a tall fern to a marble column to a sunglasses stall.

It was going well until, just outside the camera store, Brendan looked back over his shoulder. Ivy was next to a booth selling self-help books, so she ducked behind it. An old woman with a wart on her chin, sitting on the stool and tending the booth, looked at her.

Ivy smiled like nothing was abnormal, but then she noticed a security guard on the other side of the walkway staring at her. He pointed two stubby fingers at her, and then pointed them at his own eyes. *I'm watching you*, he was saying.

Ivy immediately straightened up and tried to

look innocent by grabbing one of the books from the display and opening it to a random page. *Bald is Beautiful!* it declared in large print.

Ivy panicked, slammed the book shut and shoved it back on the shelf.

'Can I help you?' the old lady said in a scratchy voice.

'Uh, just browsing!' Ivy turned away to check where Brendan was, but the one thing she really didn't need to happen had happened.

Brendan had disappeared!

Chapter Two

I can only feel two of my toes, Olivia thought. Ivy had been gone for half an hour and the line hadn't even started moving yet.

'Ohmigosh, I just can't believe you got to be in a movie with him!' said Janie. 'So, how come you have to wait in line with the rest of us?'

Olivia wondered if there was actual steam coming out of her ears. 'That's a very good question, Janie.'

Just then a huge collective shriek erupted from the front of the line. Olivia stood on her tiptoes to see that the doors to the bookstore had finally opened.

The line surged forward and, despite being about 200th in line, she got all the way to the front door of the store very quickly. There must have been another 200 people behind her. She tried to peer past the window display, to see if she could catch Jackson's attention – or even *see* him – but the store was so packed with people clutching copies of his new book, *Jackson's Journal*, that his signing desk was hidden from view.

'Look what he gave me!' squealed a girl who was leaving the store. She was the ice skater from the front of the line and was waving something red and heart-shaped over her head. 'It's a picture frame and he signed it: "Love, Jackson". He loves me!'

The girls still waiting for their chance to meet Jackson all crowded around her, desperate to see. Olivia got jostled around like she was holding the last purse in a sale.

Janie turned to Olivia and clutched her hands. 'I have to have one,' she said. 'I just have to!'

Olivia sighed. Even though Valentine's Day wasn't until the end of the week, this was her only chance to see Jackson before she left for Transylvania.

It doesn't matter, Olivia thought to herself. *Once I get to the front of the line and give him his V-Day present, this will all be worth it*. She touched the crinkly wrapping paper on the small box in her jacket pocket and smiled. The Valentine's present she'd bought for Jackson was silly, but sentimental. It was a little pair of ceramic cowboy boots. She'd painted a red heart on the front of both and put her initials on one and his initials on the other. The first thing she'd ever said to Jackson was, 'Yeehaw' and 'I like your boots' and he teased her about it all the time.

'Could you stop *mooning*?' said an impatient girl behind her.

Olivia blinked and realised the line had moved way inside the store.

'Sorry.' She scurried forwards into a wider aisle with ropes down either side. At the far end, she could see a big pink backdrop and could just catch a glimpse of Jackson's blond hair. When she caught up to the line, Janie turned around with tears in her eyes.

'Oh, no,' Olivia said, reaching to give the girl a hug. 'What's wrong?'

Janie held out her fist and opened it, palm up. The candy heart was still there but the message now read, 'I EAR U.' The letters had smudged off in her sweaty hand.

She sniffled. 'What am I going to give him now?'

Even though it was weird to have so many people obsessed with her boyfriend, Olivia couldn't let Janie be upset. She spotted a bunch of construction paper pink hearts taped up on one of the book displays. She looked both ways, to make sure no one was watching, and gently pulled off one of the smaller hearts.

Janie watched, her bottom lip trembling.

Olivia dug in her bag and pulled out a black pen. 'We've got this.' She held up the heart. 'And this.' She held up the pen. 'And we've got about five minutes for you to write something for Jackson on it.'

Janie's eyes lit up. 'Thanks!' She took the pen and the heart and wrote, 'I ❤ YOU,' in the middle. She spent the following four minutes admiring it.

'Next!' called a woman in a dark green tailored suit with an orange silk scarf. It was Amy Teller, Jackson's manager.

Janie took a deep breath and stepped up to the table. Olivia watched as Jackson turned his

19660

full attention to her, giving a trademark wide white smile.

'Hello. What's your name?' he asked. His attention was fully on the little girl and he'd totally failed to see that Olivia was next in line. She couldn't help smiling to herself. *He's so good to his fans.*

Janie was clutching the little pink paper heart so hard she was crushing it.

'J-Janie,' she replied, then thrust the heart out to him.

'Thank you,' Jackson said, his blond hair flopping over his blue eyes as he read it. 'That's really sweet.'

'I messed up your first present,' Janie confessed and stepped to the side, pointing at Olivia. 'She helped me.'

Jackson looked over and Olivia felt her heart cartwheel. He half stood up and leaned over the desk, almost knocking a pile of books over but not taking his eyes off her. She felt a flush of excitement and her heart raced.

'Olivia!' He looked happy but confused. 'What are you doing here?'

'Remember, I said last night . . .' Olivia began, wanting to give him a hug but feeling like it would be inappropriate.

Jackson winced. 'You totally did. I'm really sorry! Why didn't you call?'

'I tried,' Olivia replied, glad that it was all over now and she could talk to her boyfriend at last.

Amy Teller, Jackson's manager, was talking to a man at Jackson's shoulder. 'What do you mean, we've run out?' She was towering over one of the store's employees. His face was bright red.

'We just didn't expect this many girls,' the short man in thick-rimmed glasses replied.

'That's right,' Amy drawled, 'because a visit

from an A-list movie star is so yesterday, isn't it?'
She threw her hands up and leaned over to Janie.
'I'm sorry, sweetie,' she said, in a fake syrupy
voice, 'but we don't have any more of Jackson's
Valentine's photo frames.'

Janie's eyes filled with tears again.

'But she's been waiting in line forever,'
Olivia said.

'No more?' Janie echoed in disbelief.

'Don't be upset,' Jackson said.

Olivia looked at him pointedly. 'She's *really*
been looking forward to seeing you.'

'OK, wait there a minute,' Jackson said,
pointing to a couple of empty chairs behind
him. Then he leapt up on to the table and called
out to the rest of the line, 'Everyone, I'm really
sorry to say that we've run out of the Valentine's
photo frames.'

The crowd sighed with disappointment.

'But,' he went on, 'my pen hasn't run out of ink and I'll be here until I've signed every last one of your copies of *Jackson's Journal*.'

Everyone burst into cheers.

'Will you sit with Janie for a minute?' Jackson said to Olivia, touching her hand gently. 'We can talk after this.'

He sat back down and motioned for the girl behind Olivia to come over.

Olivia sighed. *More waiting.* She sank into the chair next to a very excited Janie.

'Oh my goodness,' she whispered. 'This is so cool! I'm hanging out with Jackson Caulfield!'

Idly, Olivia picked up a copy of *Jackson's Journal* from one of the displays on either side of the line. It had photos of the small town where he was from, pictures of him as a baby and all about his movie career. It mentioned *The Groves*, but there wasn't any mention of Olivia.

'Amy?' she asked. 'How come I'm not in here?'

Amy rolled her eyes. 'Do you have any idea how long it takes to make a book?' she replied. 'They'd finished writing it before he'd ever met you. Besides, having a girlfriend isn't good for his image.' She swept her hand out over the line of girls still waiting to get their books signed. 'Think of all the broken hearts.'

What about my *heart?* Olivia thought.

She watched the next person, a girl about Olivia's age with cropped brown hair wearing a T-shirt from *The Right One* movie.

'Happy Valentine's Day,' Jackson said to her with a smile.

He hasn't even said Happy Valentine's to me, Olivia realised.

Girl after girl came up and received the full focus of Jackson's attention for at least a minute – more than Olivia had – and walked away happy.

At last, there were only three people left in line: two teenage girls and one older woman carrying her dog, with a studded dog collar that spelled out Jackson's name.

When he was finished, Jackson turned to Olivia and Janie. 'Well, now,' he said, with a wink. 'My two favourite Valentines.'

But before he could say anything more, Amy picked up her big grey handbag. 'That was great. Now, just say a quick goodbye and we'll get you to the VIP party.'

Olivia's stomach lurched. 'You never told me about the VIP party,' she said, trying to control her emotions in front of Janie, who was listening to every word.

'I forgot. I'm sorry,' Jackson said, looking pained. He touched her hand again. 'Look, if you'll just hold on —'

'I can't,' Olivia said. *And after hours of waiting*

already, I shouldn't have to! 'Ivy has been waiting for me to leave; we've got to finish packing.'

Jackson looked unhappy. 'I wanted to see you before you went away.'

'That's why I came,' Olivia said. She wished that everything between them wasn't always so fleeting. She pulled out the box she'd wrapped in crinkly silver paper and handed it to him. 'Happy Valentine's Day.'

He took it and gave her a huge hug. For a moment, it felt like everything in the world was just how it should be. 'Thank you.'

He carefully unwrapped the paper and opened the little box. He pulled out the pair of cowboy boots and grinned.

'Yeehaw,' Olivia said quietly.

Jackson smiled, looking right into her eyes. She knew that he totally got her present. *Maybe the waiting was a little worth it*, Olivia thought.

'Those are so cute!' declared Janie, peering at the cowboy boots. 'They look just like yours, Jackson.'

'They do, don't they?' Jackson replied.

He looked from the boots to Janie and then to Olivia. She realised without him saying a word what he was thinking.

'You don't mind, do you?' Jackson asked.

Olivia was torn. It was really sweet for Jackson to give Janie something so special – but it was his Valentine's present. *Why doesn't he want to keep it for himself?* Olivia thought.

Still, she wanted Janie to leave happy and knew that was all Jackson was trying to do. She shook her head and he handed one over to a beaming Janie.

'And I'll always keep the other one very close to my heart,' Jackson said, holding up the one with Olivia's initials on it.

'You two are the best!' Janie shouted, giving Jackson and then Olivia huge hugs. 'I think you make the perfect couple,' she whispered and skipped out of the store.

'Jackson,' Amy warned. 'We have to go now.'

'I'm really sorry,' Jackson said to Olivia. 'Your present isn't . . . uh . . . ready yet. You know Valentine's isn't until the end of the week . . .' he trailed off.

Olivia tried to smile. 'It's fine, don't worry.' But inside she felt like this morning had been nothing but a big disappointment. 'We'll see each other when I get back from Transylvania.'

'If not before,' Jackson said. He gave her a hug and squeezed her hand. 'I'm really sorry about today.'

'*Jackson*,' Amy insisted.

'Bye,' Olivia said quietly.

'Bye.' He waved as he walked away.

She was about to spend yet another week away from Jackson in Transylvania, and he didn't even seem to care that much. As she walked out of the store, past the rows of Jackson Caulfield books, DVDs and posters, Olivia felt like a deflated balloon.

Might as well go home and finish packing for the trip, she thought, *but where's Ivy?* It had almost been two hours since she'd seen her sister. Olivia pulled out her phone and pushed redial.

The phone rang twice and Ivy picked up. Then Olivia heard a crash and a squeal. She yelped, holding the phone away from her ear.

'That sounded painful!'

🦇   🦇   🦇

Operation Night Stalker was well under way. Ivy had wrapped her black scarf over her head like a ninja and she was peering around a shelf of shoes.

Her suspect was ten feet due north, staring intently at a row of belts hanging on pegs.

She'd trailed him through Midnight Clothing, the Sweet Tooth candy shop and George's Glass Emporium but he still hadn't bought anything. Now, he was in Batty for Beads, the accessory store, and was looking baffled by the huge range of bags, shoes, jewellery and belts.

'Can I help you?'

The voice behind her made Ivy jump.

'Uh, no,' Ivy mumbled to the store assistant. 'Just looking, thanks.'

Brendan moved out of sight.

Drat, Ivy thought. *I'm going to have to follow.*

She flattened her back against the end of the shoe shelf and leaned out briefly, like a SWAT team member about to storm a building.

Clear, Ivy thought. *Go, go, go!*

She crouched down and scurried to the end of

the aisle. She had no idea which way he'd gone, so she grabbed a pocket mirror off the shelf in front of her and held it out, tilting it this way and that.

Bingo.

Brendan was over by a rack of necklaces and browsing through the semi-precious stone section. He picked up a long strand of chunky blue lapis lazuli with silver beads.

Ooh, thought Ivy. *That's a good one.*

Focus! she berated herself. *Don't lose sight of the mission.* She darted behind a stack of turntable shelves of beads where she could see most of the store.

Brendan was engrossed in the necklaces but, out of the corner of her eye, Ivy saw the security guard who had warned her earlier. He was walking through the entrance of the store and looking around.

I've been rumbled, Ivy thought, pulling the black scarf further over her face. She wondered if she should abandon the mission, but Brendan had three necklaces in his hand and seemed to be finally making a decision.

The security guard stopped to talk to the store assistant, who pointed back towards the shoes where Ivy was a moment ago.

'She's over there, Hank,' Ivy heard her say.

Now Brendan was moving towards the counter and Hank was approaching Ivy's hiding place. If she fled now, she'd miss whatever Brendan was going to buy, but if she didn't, her cover would be blown and she might end up in mall prison.

Before she could move, her phone blared out the tune of 'Double Trouble'. *Olivia*. Then several things happened at once . . .

Ivy panicked and fumbled for her phone.

Brendan started to turn around.

Hank spotted Ivy, his eyes widening.

She turned away just as she pressed the green button on her phone, desperately trying to silence it. Her foot hit the bottom of the bead display and her bag swung behind her, knocking into one of the layers of multi-coloured beads, making a great racket. She twisted back, trying to stop her bag hitting it again. Out of the corner of her eye, Ivy saw Brendan look over just as she went over on her ankle and wobbled into the rack. She tried to hold the display steady, only to tip the whole thing on top of her, crashing to the ground with a squeal, and sending little plastic globs of circles, squares and heart-shapes everywhere.

Lying on her back, surrounded by a rainbow of little plastic beads, Ivy felt like a smudge of black paint across a Picasso.

Brendan ran over to her. 'Are you OK?' he gasped.

Hank's face loomed. 'Gotcha!'

The store assistant shook her head at the mess.

'Uh, I'm OK.' Ivy scrambled to her feet and started collecting the beads. 'I'm really sorry; I didn't mean to.' She realised her phone was still in her hand. 'I'll call you back,' she whispered to her sister and hung up.

Hank stood there with his arms crossed and Brendan hurried to help the store assistant lift up the display rack.

'This is going to take me hours,' the assistant said.

'No, no,' Ivy replied. 'I'll do it.'

'We'll do it,' said Brendan. He crouched down among the beads and started to sort them into piles.

Ivy sat next to him, picking out the four-leaf

clover beads, completely embarrassed.

'You sure you want to help this girl who was trying to mug you?' Hank asked Brendan.

Brendan smiled. 'She wasn't trying to mug me, sir. She's my girlfriend.'

That completely baffled Hank, but at least he and the store assistant left them to their sorting.

'What's going on?' Brendan asked as he scooped all the alphabet beads into one of the lower racks.

Ivy opened her mouth to try to explain without actually confessing what she was doing, but nothing came to mind. 'Uh, well, Brendan. Honestly?' Ivy said. 'I was stalking you.'

Brendan chuckled.

She explained how she saw him and, when he lied about where he was, she guessed he might be shopping for Valentine's. 'I didn't want to be caught out as a neglectful girlfriend if you bought me a present,' she said.

'I know you're not into the cheesy pink hearts stuff, but I wanted to get you something,' Brendan said, looking embarrassed. 'Especially because you're gone the whole week of Valentine's.'

Ivy felt her heart warm up. 'Even though I made a complete bunny of myself in there, is the offer still open?'

Brendan nodded.

'Because that lapis lazuli necklace was killer.'

Brendan grinned and let a bunch of daisy-shaped beads clatter into their slot. 'Just promise me you'll give up on the spy game,' he said, smiling. 'You're not very good at it.'

Ivy nodded gratefully. 'I promise.'

Maybe Valentine's isn't so cheesy after all, Ivy thought.

🦇   🦇   🦇

Olivia was packing. Six casual outfits for the trip to Transylvania lay spread out on her four-poster bed, with her more formal outfits hanging from the antique full-length mirror in the corner.

'Is that enough?' she asked herself. 'Or one more skirt?'

Something small and white flew through her bedroom door and landed on her baby-blue pea coat. Olivia picked up the papery globe. It was a clove of garlic.

Mrs Abbott poked her head through the doorway with a silly grin on her face. 'You'll need that to fight off all the vampires in Transylvania,' she said.

Olivia forced herself to smile. 'Ha ha!' she replied weakly. Her adoptive mom and dad had no idea about her biological family's unusual eating habits and preference for sleeping in coffins. That was the First Law of the Night: *no one* could find out vampires really existed. Olivia was a rare human exception, and she was certain her mother wouldn't let her get within a mile of Transylvania if she knew the truth.

'Can I come in, honey?' Mrs Abbott asked.

'Sure,' Olivia said, tossing back the clove of garlic and sorting through her accessories. 'If you promise not to comment on the state of my room.'

'I just wanted to say again that we're so glad you've found your biological family.' Olivia heard her mom's voice crack. She glanced up and noticed that her mom had tears in her eyes. 'Your dad and I are completely supportive of this trip you're taking.'

Olivia gave her mom a big hug. 'You and Dad are my parents, and Grammy and Pops are the best grandparents a girl could have.' She didn't want anyone in her family thinking she was trying to replace them. She'd already figured out how to avoid the confusion of having two dads. Her dad, the one who'd raised her from a baby was 'Dad', while her biological dad was 'Bio-dad'. 'I just want to find out more about where I came from.'

'I know, sweetie.' Olivia's mom sat on the bed. 'Now, close your eyes.'

'Um, OK.' She closed her eyes and a moment later felt cool metal on her palm.

Olivia squinted from behind her eyelashes and squealed. It was a slim-line pink cell phone. *Super* pink.

'You're the best, Mom.' Olivia hugged her again.

When they finally broke apart, Mrs Abbott said, 'We bought international texting, so you can text us anytime you want to.'

'I will every night,' Olivia promised.

There was the sudden ring of an incoming

call. Olivia jumped with fright and the mobile phone flew up into the air. She only just managed to catch it before it hit the side of her vanity table.

Cheerleading agility 1, over-active imagination 0, Olivia thought.

Olivia looked down at her shiny new present, amazed that anyone could have the new number already. But it was her bedroom phone that was ringing.

'Hello?' Olivia said, as her mom gave a little wave and left her to her privacy.

'T-minus twelve hours,' Ivy said.

'I know,' Olivia replied. 'I'm almost done packing. How's your, um, backside?'

After Olivia heard Ivy squealing on the phone at the mall, Ivy had called back. They'd arranged to meet up and as they'd walked to the Meat and Greet she'd explained the whole story about her undercover espionage – and the unfortunate incident with the jewellery rack. Olivia had dropped the newly converted Valentine's Day lovebirds at the diner while she'd come straight home for her packing session.

'Still sore,' Ivy confessed. 'I just hope it doesn't have little heart shapes imprinted on it forever.'

Olivia laughed. 'So, are you packed?' she asked.

'I'm, um, making progress,' Ivy said.

'You mean, you've finally dragged your suitcase down from the closet and are calling me to drag your feet even more?' Olivia guessed.

'You know me too well,' Ivy admitted. 'But there is method in my madness. I just wanted to confess that you were right.'

Olivia pretended to gasp. 'Me? Right?'

'Ha ha,' Ivy said. 'You were right in saying that Valentine's Day isn't that bad and getting surprise presents is very nice.'

Olivia felt her stomach twist. 'Getting surprise presents *is* nice,' she replied quietly. *Jackson hasn't even given me a* card.

'Uh oh,' Ivy said. 'I can hear you not-smiling.'

Olivia stroked her soft silver cashmere-mix sweater and sighed.

'I'm just worried about being homesick when we get to Transylvania,' Olivia said, deciding that bringing up Jackson would only take away from Ivy's happy Brendan feelings.

'Don't you worry,' Ivy said. 'We are bound to have an amazing time, and everyone is going to make us feel right at home.'

'I'm sure *you'll* be right at home,' Olivia replied, imagining shadowy castles, fog and mist, vampires that might be old enough to remember what it was like to actually eat humans . . . gulp.

'This is your family too, Olivia,' Ivy insisted. 'They are going to love us both equally. Just you wait. Now, the black roll-neck sweater or the skull-design hooded top? Which do you think?'

Olivia laughed. 'You'll look perfect in either,' she told her sister. As she put the phone down and put the last few items in her suitcase, she felt a jangle of nerves in her stomach.

Tomorrow, she would be in Transylvania.

Chapter Three

Ivy stepped into the Arrivals lounge, bright and bustling with people chattering in Romanian. She felt as fresh as a daisy – or as a vampire who'd slept well in their coffin.

Poor Olivia, though, seemed frazzled beyond recognition. Her eyes were the same colour pink as her sweater and her normally healthy-looking skin looked almost as white as a vampire's. She'd barely slept a wink.

'I'll take care of your passports, girls,' said Mr Vega from behind her, wheeling his suitcase.

'Oh my darkness, I can't believe we're finally

here,' Ivy said, passing hers over.

'How long until we get to the house?' Olivia mumbled, her eyes drooping. She stumbled and her bag's wheels clattered on the shiny tile floor.

'You can sleep in the car, my dear,' Mr Vega replied, putting his arm around Olivia's shoulder and giving her a squeeze.

Ivy stopped short. An unusually tall man in an all-black uniform and an old-fashioned driving cap was holding a sign that said 'Olivia + Ivy'.

She hurried over. 'We're Olivia plus Ivy!' she announced.

The man tipped his hat. 'I am honoured to be first to say *welcome*, beautiful Miss Ivy.' He took Ivy's suitcase out of her hand. 'I'm Horatio, Lazar family butler for four generations. And this must be lovely Miss Olivia?'

'You speak English!' Ivy blurted, knowing straight away how rude she sounded. Her face coloured. 'I'm sorry,' she said, 'I wasn't sure if anyone would be able to.'

Horatio smiled. 'In our town everyone is taught English from a young age.' He pulled his shoulders back as he beamed with pride. 'We have an excellent education system here.'

'I can see that,' Ivy said, wondering how long it would take her to learn Romanian.

'You aren't wearing a cowboy hat,' Horatio said, peering at Olivia and frowning.

'Um . . .' Olivia looked as confused as Ivy felt.

'Oh ho ho!' Horatio chuckled deeply, like Santa Claus. 'I'm joking! All Americans on TV wear cowboy hats.'

Ivy realised he was trying to be friendly and grinned when Horatio shook their hands gravely.

Horatio turned to their dad. 'Welcome home, Mr Lazar.' He picked up both the girls' fully packed suitcases with one arm.

'Please, Horatio, call me Charles, Charles *Vega*.' Ivy could see her dad was feeling uncomfortable. He kept running a hand through his hair. Her dad hadn't spoken to his family in years and he'd changed his identity entirely just to avoid them. Ivy hoped this trip wasn't going to be too awkward for him.

'It's great to meet you, Mr Horatio,' Ivy said. 'I hope you'll tell us stories about when Dad was our age and getting into trouble.'

Horatio's face broke into a grin, revealing teeth as crooked as abandoned gravestones. 'Once, on a visit to the palace, I caught him smuggling one of Queen's pet ferrets –'

'That is enough of that story, Horatio!'

Ivy grinned as her normally composed dad actually *blushed*. 'I think we are all keen to bring this journey to an end,' she said.

Horatio tipped his hat again and resumed his

serious expression. But while her dad was putting their passports into his briefcase, Horatio leant down and whispered, 'I'll tell you the rest later.'

Ivy smiled and slipped her arm through Horatio's. He led her out into the chilly Romanian afternoon. She could just make out the tops of mountains in the distance, well beyond the airport.

Waiting outside, being ignored by the attendant shooing away other parked cars, was a sleek grey four-by-four with black-tinted windows. Horatio opened the door and Ivy saw soft leather seats and two velvety blankets for her and Olivia to stay warm under.

'Ooh,' Olivia said appreciatively and climbed inside.

It was a little bit more . . . formal . . . than Ivy was expecting, but she followed her sister.

Once they were tucked in, Horatio poured

them both a cup of hot tea from a Thermos. Ivy shifted in her seat and banged her hand against the side of the door, leaving a little line where the metal claw of her ring scratched the leather.

Ivy gulped. As her dad got into the front seat, she sat stiffly, trying not to move so she wouldn't ruin anything else. *I'm not used to this luxurious lifestyle*, she thought. *And it's not used to me.*

Five minutes later, Olivia was snoring lightly. As they drove, the city buildings turned into lush countryside. Ivy had never seen anything so beautiful. Deep green grass stretched for miles into the distance, where the sharp, snow-covered mountains loomed. The car followed a sparkling, slow-moving river and then drove through a village where the closely-packed houses were painted bright red, yellow and blue. They glided past stone mansions and rustic inns. Ivy felt like she had been whisked into a magical fairytale land.

But I'm no princess, she thought. She tried to reassure herself: *I suppose I'll adjust.*

After an hour and a half, they turned on to a road that cut through a thick forest. Trees towered over the car like the vaulted ceiling of a cathedral. They blocked out the sun and it was almost as if it were already night.

Olivia woke up as the road narrowed and got bumpy.

Mr Vega twisted in his seat and gave them a tense smile. 'We do not have far to go now, my daughters.'

Ivy hadn't been worried before, but with the butler and the fancy car, she was feeling like she wasn't really prepared to meet her family. What if she kept making a mess? Or she said the wrong thing? She hadn't really thought what being related to a Count and Countess meant.

Olivia reached out for her sister's hand and Ivy was glad for the millionth time that she had her twin by her side.

When we left I was trying to perk up Olivia, Ivy thought. *Now I'm the one feeling jumpy.*

'Before we arrive,' Mr Vega said, 'I want to say something. The three of us are a family and I will never let anything come between us again.'

Ivy saw Horatio glance over at her dad.

Maybe the same goes for the Count and Countess? Ivy hoped. She'd love it if her dad and his parents were able to put their differences behind them.

Moments later, Horatio turned the car down a tree-lined lane and paused at tall iron gates that swung open automatically. They then rolled up the long, sloping drive.

'That is the vineyard, dormant for winter.' Horatio pointed out of the left window at neat rows of wooden frames with brown vines clinging to them. 'And the stables are on the right. I'm afraid the lake house at the back of the property is closed but you might get a chance to skate on the frozen lake.'

The lake house! Ivy mouthed to her sister.

Then, the house came into view.

'How old is this place?' Ivy asked, staring up at the six towers casting imposing shadows across the lawn.

'Only three hundred years old,' Horatio said dismissively.

It was even bigger than the gothic building that housed the entire Franklin Grove Middle School. The dozens of windows along the long facade were dark and uninviting. As they came to a stop, Ivy could see gargoyles on the rooftop. They seemed to stare down disapprovingly. Normally, Ivy would be all about the gargoyles, but she was feeling so out of place.

She followed her sister out of the car and the cold made her shiver. Her clunky boots crunched on the gravel, and she saw that the door knocker was a distorted face with fangs.

Ivy shuddered. *I'm a long way from home*, she thought. *A very long way.*

Olivia expected the huge oak doors to creak open, but they swung open silently.

It was warm inside and the scent of burning pine logs filled the air from the open fireplace in the corner of the hallway.

'It's almost cosy,' she whispered to Ivy, who was gazing up at the walls.

Olivia followed her gaze to see portraits of stern-looking men and women. One woman was wearing a tight corset and a large ruby ring on her finger while another stared down at them dressed in a velvet cloak and white ruff. They all had pale skin and unusual-coloured eyes.

'This must be the family,' Ivy said.

Opposite the front door and to both sides were long corridors, making a T-shape. Each corridor was decorated with tapestries, chandeliers and more paintings. 'It's like a museum,' Olivia whispered.

From the hall on the right, an elderly couple dressed in black entered the room. Olivia caught her breath. The woman was graceful and elegant. Olivia immediately felt dishevelled and under-dressed. Her hair was in a neat bun and she wore a stunning green jewel on a choker. Olivia realised it was shaped like an eye with a V in the middle – the same symbol that was on her and Ivy's matching rings. This must be her grandmother, the Countess.

'Welcome home, Karl,' she said. She held out

her hand, her arm clad in intricate black lace, for Mr Vega to kiss.

Olivia couldn't help noticing how her father's face coloured. 'It is Charles, now, Mother,' he replied stiffly. 'Call me Charles.'

'Yes, of course,' the Countess said, drawing back. 'I'm sorry.' She looked hopefully into Charles's face. 'It's good to have you back.' Her voice was thick with emotion.

At her shoulder, the Count cleared his throat loudly and wiped his eyes. 'Just a . . . speck of soot from the fire,' he muttered.

'It's good to be back,' Mr Vega said, after a moment. 'Though this will all take some getting used to.' He tried to laugh but it came out as a croak.

The Count shook his son's hand awkwardly and then fiddled with his thick grey moustache.

There was an uncomfortable pause, until the

Countess turned to Olivia and Ivy. 'And you must be our beautiful granddaughters. We are so happy to meet you at long, long last.' She hurried forwards with a smile and her arms opened wide for a warm hug.

As she released them, their grandfather approached. Beneath his waxed moustache, Olivia could just see his mouth split in a grin. 'Darling children!' he said. Olivia shared a glance with Ivy, and then the two of them stepped into his arms. His suit rustled noisily next to their ears, and Olivia could feel the thick wool scratching her.

She took a deep breath and pulled away. Looking at the sparkling eyes of the Count and the Countess, and the smile on her sister's face, Olivia knew Ivy was right: this was their family and even if she was different, she was sure she could still belong here.

'Welcome home,' said the Countess. 'Do you like our little abode?'

Olivia found herself smiling from ear to ear. 'It's perfect,' she said, gazing around. 'Just perfect!'

🦇　　　　🦇　　　　🦇

'Would you like a tour?' the Countess said, taking each girl by the hand. Her fingers were heavy with jewellery.

Ivy hesitated before nodding. She definitely wanted to see the rest of this amazing place but she couldn't help but notice that every time she took a step, the sound of her heels striking the floorboards echoed loudly. Too loudly? *Why can't I just relax?* she wondered.

'Let's see if you can remember your way around, Kar– er, Charles,' said the Count, slapping Mr Vega on the back and smiling.

'Girls, this is the parlour,' the Countess said,

opening the door to a sunny room with white and cream wallpaper, blue velvet chairs and a white baby grand piano in the corner. A delicate golden chandelier hung from the ceiling and light yellow curtains framed the tall windows.

'Wow,' Olivia breathed.

'It hasn't changed much,' Mr Vega commented.

'Some things have,' the Countess said softly. 'You see that vase?' She turned back to the hall and pointed to a simple, tall piece of green ceramic shaped like a V on its own little table. 'I never used to like modern pieces, but this one I could not resist.'

'Very nice,' Mr Vega commented. Ivy should have guessed that her grandparents would appreciate the artistic as much as her dad.

Ivy reached out to stroke the varnish – only noticing too late that her dad was bending over to peer more closely. Her elbow connected with his nose and, with a yelp of pain, he staggered forwards, right into the vase's table.

'Oh no!' gasped their grandmother as Olivia shrieked.

The vase wobbled then toppled, but Ivy managed to twist her body to the left and catch it before it hit the floor.

'It's OK!' Ivy called. 'All fine.' Her heart was racing. 'I'm so sorry.'

'Don't worry.' The Countess gingerly took the vase and placed it back on the table. 'There we are,' she said. 'No damage done.'

Ivy smiled weakly. *Stake me now*, she thought.

'Your house is so beautiful,' Olivia said, trying to distract everyone, as they followed their grandmother further down the hall. 'What's wrong?' she mouthed to Ivy when no one was watching.

Ivy shrugged. How could she tell her sister

how awkward she was feeling, when Olivia was clearly having the time of her life?

'Thank you, my dear,' their grandmother said, 'but you must remember that this is your house, too.'

Ivy saw Olivia beam, but couldn't feel the same. Not while she was walking around as gracefully as Frankenstein's monster wearing a blindfold.

'Here is the kitchen,' the Countess said. She pushed through a wooden swing door to an enormous room with a low ceiling that was humming with preparations – people were chopping, slicing and dicing. Ivy counted five pots bubbling away on two stoves. A large woman with a smudge of flour on her cheek bustled over. 'Madam,' she said.

'Greta, these are my grandchildren,' said the Countess.

The woman peered at them. 'Such skinny girls!'

'Greta is our head chef,' the Countess said.

'Nice to meet you,' Olivia and Ivy said at the same time.

'And she makes the best beef stroganoff in Romania,' said Mr Vega from the back of the group.

Greta gasped. 'My mititei!'

The Count chuckled. 'She's always called him that,' he said to the twins. 'It means "little sausage".'

Ivy couldn't help laughing with her sister.

Greta pushed past everyone to squish Mr Vega in a hug. 'Are you hungry? What can I make for you?'

Mr Vega laughed. 'Nothing, Greta. Thank you. I am saving room for dinner.'

Greta clapped her big hands and hurried back to the kitchen table. She picked up a rolling pin and waved it in the air. 'Yes, tonight! Everything is prepared for your formal dinner this evening, Madam, including the vegetarian meal.'

'F-formal?' Ivy stuttered.

'Of course, my darling,' the Countess replied. 'We are keen to introduce Ka– Charles back into society, and present his gorgeous daughters. Tonight is just a little dinner for thirty.'

'Thirty!' Ivy said. As the Countess continued to direct the staff, Ivy whispered to Olivia, 'I didn't know! I didn't bring anything.'

Olivia's eyes widened. 'Your dad did say . . .'

Ivy closed her eyes, picturing the sniggers if she came to dinner in one of her Goth outfits. She'd brought some nice clothes, but nothing *formal*. The word made her cringe.

'Don't worry,' Olivia whispered. 'You can borrow one of mine.'

Ivy sighed. Olivia had everything under

control, and Ivy couldn't help feeling like she stuck out like cotton candy at a funeral.

🦇   🦇   🦇

'Come, my granddaughters,' the Countess said. 'I shall show you to your coffin room.'

Olivia was loving every minute of their tour. Greta seemed really nice, and Olivia had already decided to call her dad a little sausage at some point.

The hallway from the kitchens opened up to a spiral staircase. Olivia guessed it must lead to one of the round towers she'd seen when they were approaching the house. Paintings of forests and castles were hung on the walls and ornate vases stood in little alcoves. As they ascended, Olivia noticed that the dark wooden hand rail had the family symbol carved into it. On the next floor, heavy scarlet curtains with golden tassels framed the window, which showed glimpses of the lake and gardens with hedges in long curving patterns.

Olivia felt like she was on a movie set, every-thing was so immaculate and extravagant. That idea gave her heart a pang. *What's Jackson doing now?* she wondered.

After the stairs had curved past four flights, Grandmother stopped at a door. 'I thought you might like to share a suite.'

She pushed open the door to reveal two four-poster beds with billowing white curtains in the middle of an enormous attic room. A pair of large antique wardrobes faced each other and matching desks with computers were tucked into two corners. Their suitcases had already arrived.

'It's so beautiful!' Olivia whispered.

'Tessa, one of our maids, will help you with anything you may need.' The Countess pointed to a cord near the door. 'Just pull on this.'

'How many people work here?' Ivy asked.

'Well, we have two maids, a valet, Greta the chef and one assistant, a groundskeeper and, of course, Horatio is our butler, but he's really more like family.' The Countess smiled. 'And we are all going to make sure you have a wonderful time this week.' She swept both of them up in another hug. 'I'm just so delighted to have you here.'

She left swiftly, shutting the door behind her, and Olivia flitted from one piece of furniture to the next.

'This totally sucks!' Olivia exclaimed with a grin, knowing her sister would get the vampire terminology for 'totally awesome'. 'It's even better than I could have imagined.'

But when she saw the look on her sister's face, Olivia hurried to the bed where Ivy was perched.

'What's wrong?' she asked.

'I stick out like a spider on a ballet shoe,' Ivy confessed. 'I mean, that vase . . . and did you hear my boots clunking with every step?'

Olivia laughed. 'Those boots make a great racket whenever you wear them – and you didn't break the vase.'

Ivy shook her head. 'It's different here. They have servants! And this formal dinner . . .'

Before Olivia could stop her, Ivy unzipped her suitcase and started rifling through clothes. 'Wrong, wrong . . . No good . . . No!' Ivy declared pulling things out. She pulled out her sweatshirt that said 'Do I scare you?' with a cute little cartoon of Dracula underneath.

Olivia chuckled but Ivy wailed, 'Why do all my clothes have stupid slogans on them?'

Olivia knelt down and gently took her sister's hands. 'Calm down. It's all going to be fine. You just need to relax.'

Olivia took Ivy over to her suitcase and opened it up. She took out the garment bag where she'd packed several nice outfits and pulled away a pink knee-length dress, a green empire waist dress and a light blue sleeveless ballerina-style skirt.

'Those are all pretty,' Ivy admitted. 'But they are utterly you.'

'Luckily . . .' Olivia paused for dramatic effect. 'I have this!' Underneath the ballerina skirt was another one, darker blue and floor-length with a corset waist and cap sleeves.

Ivy reached out and tentatively stroked the embroidered hem.

'But does it come in black?' Ivy asked.

'You can totally rock this dress,' Olivia declared. 'Black or not.'

'OK.' Ivy took the blue dress and held it up to her body, running her hand down the fabric. 'You're right.'

Ivy unzipped the dress and started to try it on,

but from her sister's frown, Olivia could tell Ivy was still worrying.

'Ivy, remember what you told me?' Olivia said.

'Don't let the coffin bugs bite?' she replied, zipping up the side and twirling in the mirror.

'This is our family,' Olivia reminded her, 'and they are going to love us just the way we are.'

Ivy took a deep breath and Olivia could tell she was forcing her smile. 'You're right. They will love me just the way I am . . . while I'm wearing one of your dresses.'

How weird, Olivia thought as she started to get ready herself. *It was supposed to be me feeling like I didn't fit in, not Ivy.*

Chapter Four

A little less than an hour later, Ivy teetered at the top of a steep, twisting stone staircase.

How can I possibly survive this? Ivy thought. *Four flights of stairs in these shoes . . .* The heels weren't high, but she was used to chunky boots, not dainty slippers. She gripped the handrail and willed herself not to collapse.

In front of her, Olivia stepped confidently down the stairs in her pink dress and silver Grecian sandals.

Ivy took a first tentative step, holding up the short train of satiny fabric that trailed behind the borrowed blue dress, and her ankle wobbled.

'These shoes are impossible!' Ivy declared, stopping.

Olivia turned back a few steps below her. 'Just remember, toe first, not heel.'

'I'm trying!' Ivy replied.

What's more embarrassing? Ivy thought, wishing Olivia had let her wear her own shoes. *Boots with formal wear or falling flat on my face?*

'What if I get it all wrong?' Ivy said. 'What if I embarrass Dad in front of everyone?'

Olivia looked up at her. 'You won't. Besides, I'll be right by your side the whole time. Now, come on.'

'Good evening,' Horatio said from the bottom of the last staircase, making Ivy jump. 'May I show you to the drawing room?'

'Yes, please,' Olivia said.

More like show me to the firing squad, Ivy thought

but followed anyway.

'The guests have already arrived, including the Queen.' Horatio led them back through the entrance hall and down one of the other long corridors.

Olivia gasped. 'The Queen?'

Ivy stumbled in shock and nearly twisted her ankle.

They passed a fierce-looking suit of armour that was standing to attention, holding a huge battleaxe. Ivy half-expected it to come thumping after her, shouting, 'Intruder!'

The sisters walked past a pretty young girl, a little older than them, with long, black braided hair wearing a white linen apron and black dress. She was heading in the opposite direction but paused to curtsy.

Ivy stopped. 'Hi,' she said. 'I'm Ivy.'

'Um.' The girl glanced from Ivy to Olivia to

Horatio. He gave her a small nod, as though granting her permission to speak. 'Hello, miss. I'm Tessa.'

'Hi, Tessa,' Olivia said. 'Nice to meet you.'

'I love your bracelet,' Ivy said, admiring the black eyelet ribbon wound around her wrist.

Tessa smiled. 'Thanks. It isn't technically part of my uniform, but Madam doesn't mind.'

Horatio coughed lightly.

'Ah, yes. Your guests are all waiting.' Tessa curtsied again and hurried away.

'She seems nice,' Ivy said to Olivia as they walked after Horatio.

A few minutes later, Horatio paused in front of a doorway with two footmen standing on either side.

Stop worrying, Ivy, she told herself. *This is no big deal.* She paused for a moment and closed her eyes, wishing Brendan was with her.

The two footmen opened the doors at the same time and thirty pale faces turned to stare. Black dresses and sparkling jewels or dinner jackets and shiny shoes adorned people who were definitely from a different generation to Olivia and Ivy. This was the society that her grandmother wanted to introduce them to, the very top of the vampire food chain.

Chair feet scraped against polished floorboards as all the men stood up. Someone was playing the piano softly in the corner.

This is so much more formal than anywhere I've been, Ivy thought, wanting to scurry back upstairs to the safety of her room.

Ivy's glance was drawn to one woman who was sitting in a chair, wearing a silver dress. She wore several strands of pearls in a choker at her neck and watched the twins closely. Ivy could see right away that she was the Queen.

'I present Olivia Abbott and Ivy Vega,' Horatio said with a bow, and Ivy had no choice but to walk into the room. There was a moment's silence, and then everyone broke into smiles and applause.

What are they clapping for? Ivy thought. *We haven't done anything.*

Olivia dropped into a curtsy and gave Ivy a nudge to follow suit. Ivy copied her sister, and hoped she wasn't going to topple over, but the skirt of her borrowed dress got tangled up in her legs. *It's eating me alive!* she thought desperately.

The Count came over and led the sisters into the middle of the room. Ivy tried hard not to wobble in her shoes.

'This is your great-uncle Dragos and your great-aunt Elisabeta,' said the Count, introducing an elderly man in a military uniform and a lady wearing long white gloves and sparkling sapphires. 'Your great-uncle and aunt are the Viscount and Viscountess of Kolozs.'

Olivia struck up a conversation right away about the house but Ivy felt tongue-tied by all of the assured, elegant people.

'How are you doing?' the Count whispered.

'It's a little . . . um . . . more elegant than I expected,' Ivy whispered back and his grey moustache twitched up into a smile.

'Just wait until the Valentine's Day ball.' He winked at her.

Ivy gulped. *Uh oh*, she thought. *What am I going to wear to a ball?*

After Ivy had been introduced to too many people with complicated names and titles – including the Queen – the tinkle of a bell rang out.

A man wearing a dinner jacket and a red cravat announced, 'Dinner is served.'

Glasses clinked as people put them on tables and stood up.

'Isn't this so exciting?' Olivia whispered, her eyes sparkling even brighter than their great-aunt's jewels.

Ivy nodded, not wanting to spoil it for her sister.

'You look so beautiful!' the Countess whispered to Ivy, taking her elbow and walking her towards a door at the other end of the room. But before she could catch a glimpse of the dinner table, Ivy heard the room behind her suddenly fall silent.

Oh no, Ivy thought. *Did I step wrong?*

She looked back into the drawing room. Her dad stood in the entrance looking as out of place as Ivy felt.

This must be even harder for him, Ivy thought. Today was his first time back in Transylvania for more than thirteen years. After he had run away with Ivy and Olivia's human mother, his relationship had been forbidden and denounced. He had been the centre of a huge royal scandal.

Just as Ivy was about to break away from the Countess and go to stand next to him, Mr Vega strode into the dining room. He smiled at his two daughters and then bowed precisely to a man about his age wearing a grey tie and thick black glasses. The man bowed back and then they both broke into smiles. Ivy guessed that they must be old friends.

At least he's got some people on his side, Ivy thought. *And he knows how to handle all the formalities.*

As he started to make his way around the room, the Countess touched Ivy's arm. 'Those are your seats,' she said and pointed to places in the middle of a long, dark wood table that was so glossy Ivy could see the reflections of all the candles in its surface. It was decorated with red rose centrepieces, napkins folded like origami, six glasses at every place setting, plus more knives and forks by her plate than in her entire cutlery drawer at home.

There was only one thought swirling around Ivy's head: *I am so in over my coffin.*

🦇   🦇   🦇

Olivia had to pry Ivy's fingers off her arm.

'Don't leave me!' her sister hissed.

'I have to,' Olivia whispered back. 'It's boy, girl, boy, girl.' Olivia felt awful, but occasions like this required seating arrangements. 'Insisting on sitting together is worse than confusing the forks, Ivy.'

'Fine,' Ivy whispered but Olivia could tell Ivy was the complete opposite of fine.

Someone was already standing behind the chair in between the two empty ones that the

Countess had pointed to. He seemed a bit older than them with spiky black hair and high cheekbones.

'Ivy,' he said, 'and Olivia.' He bowed.

As he pulled out her chair, Olivia touched the clip holding her hair up, hoping she hadn't overdone the curls.

'I'm Alex,' he said.

'*Prince* Alex,' the Count clarified as he sat down on the other side of Ivy. 'We are delighted you could attend.'

A prince! Olivia thought as he took her hand and kissed it lightly. She was going to eat with the royal family!

Prince Alex turned to Ivy and did the same. Olivia hid her smile as Ivy's jaw dropped.

'Nice to meet you, uh, Your Highness?' Olivia said.

'Please, just call me Alex,' he replied as he sat in

his own seat. His eyes twinkled with excitement. 'You are the first American – and the first human – I have sat next to for dinner.'

Olivia was surprised. 'You've never had dinner with a human before?'

'My mother occasionally meets non-vampire dignitaries but she doesn't say much about them.' Alex lowered his voice. 'On the other hand, you and your father have been the subject of much discussion.'

Olivia felt as though a cool breeze had just blown through the room. She realised that maybe some of these vampire guests didn't approve of her. Olivia knew that there were plenty of separationists – vampires that thought humans and vampires should never mingle, and especially never have relationships. That's why her father marrying their mother had been such a scandal.

'I can assure you that I am not biased in my

views,' Alex said, looking at her intently. He leaned forward slightly. 'Your eyes are fascinating. I am used to vampire eye colours, but yours are like a sparkling summer lake.'

Olivia blushed.

Suddenly, the household staff glided into the room, carrying individual silver domed trays. Olivia smiled at the girl Tessa that they'd met in the hallway earlier, who was serving the opposite side of the table. The staff placed the plates down noiselessly in front of everyone and, with a metallic ring, lifted the domes off to reveal something the size and colour of a pot of lip balm in the centre of each large, white plate. They stood back against the walls, waiting.

Horatio bowed to the group and said simply, 'Pâté en croûte.'

Ew, Olivia thought. She was relieved to see that on her plate was a fresh garden salad.

'It looks like a rainbow,' Alex said, glancing at the vegetables.

Olivia was surprised by the description, but he was right. The red and yellow peppers, the green celery and cucumber, the purple-looking red lettuce – the colours were bright.

'You certainly have a way with words,' Olivia commented.

'Thank you,' Alex bowed his head a little. 'I do love poetry. Have you ever read "Thirteen Ways of Looking at a Blackbird" by Wallace Stevens?'

Olivia shook her head.

'You must.' Prince Alex looked wistful for a moment. 'There are so many ways to see the same thing.'

Like the meaning of Valentine's Day, Olivia thought to herself. Despite being surrounded by all these wonderful new things, a part of her heart was still with Jackson, wondering if he was thinking of her. She wanted to rush upstairs and check her new phone for texts.

As she ate her croutons, Alex said, 'I hope we will get to spend more time together while you are here in my country. There is so much I can show you, so many places to visit.'

Olivia was flattered but she heard a tut coming from across the table. Directly opposite her, the Queen was watching them with her lips pressed together.

Olivia felt a hot flush creep up her cheeks and she tried to un-blush as she concentrated on her food. *Is the Queen unhappy that her son is fraternising with a human?* Olivia wondered. Alex had kept glancing over at her while they were talking. *Is her Royal Vampness one of the ones doing the 'discussing' about vampire–human relations?*

Olivia saw Ivy leaning forward on the other side of Alex, trying to catch her attention.

Horatio suddenly appeared at Ivy's side. 'What may I do for you, Miss Ivy?'

'Uh, no, no, nothing,' Ivy mumbled. 'I was just trying to . . . um . . .'

'Ivy and I very much enjoyed our drive from the airport,' Olivia said to the prince, hoping it would be enough for him to include Ivy in their conversation.

Horatio bowed and backed away. The staff had been so quiet, Olivia had almost forgotten they were standing there.

Alex dabbed at his mouth with his napkin. 'The countryside here is underappreciated by the world's tourists, in my view. I can never get enough of it.'

'And I can't get enough of this pâté,' Ivy said. She had already finished her little portion and was munching on the watercress around the edges that everyone else was leaving untouched.

'Do you think there will be any more of it?'

Alex chuckled. 'Are you asking if you can have mine?'

Ivy winced. 'No, no. I just meant . . . I could massacre a burger right now.'

Olivia glanced around the room, suddenly aware of the silence that surrounded them. Twenty-nine other faces were turned in their direction. Ivy's exclamation had come at just the wrong time. Burgers at a formal dinner?

Olivia could see her sister struggling to swallow and Olivia had no idea what to do to save her sister.

'Oh, yes,' Alex said, loudly enough for the whole table to hear. 'Those wagyu beef burgers from Japan are such a delicacy.'

The Countess, sitting opposite them next to Mr Vega, agreed. 'When I went to visit the Imperial House of Japan, they served the most wonderful kobe beef, which is a kind of wagyu.'

Olivia let out her breath as the other vampires nodded appreciatively. Ivy shot Alex a grateful look.

For a prince, Olivia thought, *Alex seems really down-to-earth and welcoming.* His modesty reminded her of Jackson a little.

She missed Jackson. *Is he even missing me? Will he do anything at all for Valentine's Day?*

Across the table, the Queen snapped her fingers at the maid, Tessa. Olivia noticed Prince Alex watching intently. 'My water is too warm. Bring me ice,' she commanded.

'Yes, ma'am.' Tessa curtsied and hurried off.

Gosh, Olivia thought. *The Queen sure knows how to act like a royal.*

'If you like our Romanian countryside, Olivia and Ivy, I must show you our estate,' said Prince

Alex. For some reason, his face had coloured. 'Please be my guests at the palace tomorrow.'

Olivia felt a thrill. *The palace!*

She glanced across the table and saw the Queen staring back, her face impassive. Olivia gulped. It seemed that the Queen of Transylvania wasn't happy that her son was mingling with a human. Not one tiny bit.

As the rest of the courses arrived one by one, Ivy tried not to say anything. Every time she had attempted conversation, she'd said something stupid. *Olivia fits in better than me – and she's the bunny!*

Ivy was used to being around vampires, but the vampires that she knew weren't so hoity-toity. She missed Franklin Grove; she missed Brendan, she missed Sophia . . .

And to top it all off, she thought, *I'm hungry!* The food was delicious, but the portions were tiny.

'Is everything to your satisfaction, my dear?' asked the Count, wiping a drop of wine from his moustache. 'You seem unsettled.'

Ivy didn't want him to think she was too selfish to appreciate all the effort they were going to for them.

'I think it might be jet lag,' she offered.

'Of course,' he said. 'Sometimes the only thing that will revive me after a long flight is a sleep in my own coffin.' Then he whispered, 'And a formal dinner can put me in a coma!'

Ivy grinned at her grandfather's rebellious streak. She couldn't help but love him as he chuckled to himself.

He leaned in closer. 'After dessert, I could distract everyone while you and Olivia slip away?'

'What's that, Nicholas?' the Countess said with an arched eyebrow.

'Nothing, dear Caterina.' He cleared his throat.

'I want the girls to join our important guests for petits fours and coffee in the parlour after dinner,' the Countess said.

'Mother,' Mr Vega said, 'if Ivy is tired, she can be excused.'

The Countess pressed her lips together. Clearly, that wasn't an option.

Ivy stared at the table, resisting the urge to fiddle with the cutlery. She'd already drawn enough attention to herself, causing tension between their dad and his mom.

This isn't quite happy families, Ivy thought. *Not yet.*

Chapter Five

'This place is so amazing,' Olivia said as she fell back on to her four-poster bed.

The heavy velvet curtains blocked out the bright moonlight and her long-sleeved pink flannel pyjamas made her feel cosy and warm. She didn't even mind the flock of bats she'd seen flying across the moon when she was closing the curtains.

'Wasn't Prince Alex a surprise?' she said, remembering how much laughing they'd done after dinner when Olivia told him about the first time she and Ivy had switched places.

'He was the only person not horrified by my use of cutlery,' Ivy replied, tying her hair back into a ponytail. 'How did you know how to do it?'

'I saw it in a movie,' Olivia replied. 'You just work from the outside in. And you're supposed to curtsy, like, all the time around royals.'

'I figured that,' Ivy said. 'My ribs ache from all your elbowing.'

'Just trying to help my socially inept sister,' Olivia said, chuckling. 'We need to send you to finishing school.'

'Ha ha,' Ivy said. 'They're probably all talking about me and my uncivilised manners as they go home in their horse-and-carriages.'

Olivia laughed. 'No one uses horse-and-carriages any more, not even vampires!'

'Well, they don't even have cell-phone signal out here,' Ivy complained.

It was true. Olivia had practically hung out

of the window when they'd first come upstairs trying to get even one bar on her new phone, with no luck.

'You can't deny that some people in the room really didn't approve of us and our dad,' Ivy went on.

Olivia remembered the look that the Queen gave her. 'You're right, but we can't please everyone.'

Ivy grinned. 'Especially the Ice Queen.'

Olivia laughed. She crossed her eyes, looking down at her nose. 'My country is too warm. Fetch me a slab of ice.'

'Fetch me an iceberg!' Ivy put on a nasal voice and snapped her fingers impatiently.

The girls giggled together. They certainly were a long way from home.

'But at least Grandmother and Grandfather are so nice,' Olivia said.

Ivy shifted the mattress on her four-poster bed to reveal the shiny black coffin. Olivia knew that it was how vampires normally set up their rooms – a mattress for studying or, in Ivy's room, throwing clothes on, with a coffin tucked away underneath.

'The Count and Countess are just like I imagined them.' Ivy climbed into her coffin. 'I'm so glad we've been able to start putting our family back together again.'

'Me, too,' Olivia said and yawned. She snuggled into her pillow and pulled the blanket over her. 'Goodnight, Ivy.'

'Goodnight, Olivia.'

Even though it was the middle of the night, Ivy pushed open her luxurious coffin lid. It was a velvet-lined Interna Three, the best coffin money could buy. But she still couldn't sleep.

She was so *hungry*. 'Petty fors' had turned out to be delicious little chocolates. Ivy had only managed to swipe three of them. She could have eaten the whole tray.

As quietly as she could, she climbed out of the coffin and headed downstairs. Now that everyone was in bed, the house was colder, but the light of the moon and her uber-vamp eyesight meant that she could make out everything clearly.

The mansion was silent until her bare foot made a step creak. She quickly hopped to the next one, which creaked even louder.

It's like I'm walking on a giant, badly tuned piano, she thought. The portraits on the wall seemed to be frowning at her.

Finally, after four creaky flights she made it downstairs and snuck down the hall into the kitchen.

She paused, listening at the door. There was

no sound inside. *I'm sure I can unearth something in this huge kitchen*, she thought as she went in.

Her head filled with images of the wagyu burgers that Alex had described. *Mmm*, she thought, but then pushed them from her mind. *Nothing fancy, just filling.*

She tried the huge walk-in refrigerator. The doors opened to reveal shelves full of delicious-looking things to eat.

Ivy didn't want to get in more trouble by messing up a recipe or taking something she shouldn't but, to her delight, she found a box of four pieces of cold meat-lovers' pizza tucked away behind a jar of Platelet Paste and a stack of sausages. There was a note scrawled on it that read, 'For N, C mustn't see.'

Ivy chuckled to herself. Her grandfather Nicholas was trying to hide pizza from her grandmother Caterina. *I'll never tell*, Ivy thought, *as long as you don't mind me taking a piece or two.*

She pulled off two pieces and grabbed a carton of blood orange juice. Back in the relative warm of the kitchen, she sat on a stool in the dark and gobbled down her midnight feast. In the silence, Ivy looked around. The kitchen was immaculate but old. Copper pots hung from the ceiling and there were embers in the big fireplace in the middle.

As she licked the last bit of sauce off her fingers, she decided to leave a note, in case the Count wondered what had happened to his pizza. There were a few pens in a canister on the countertop, so she grabbed one, slipped back into the walk-in fridge and wrote, 'Ivy's stomach says THANK YOU!' and drew a little smiley face with fangs.

She hurried out of the kitchen but before she could head towards the stairs to her bedroom, she heard a gasping noise. Ivy froze.

Someone else is awake! In an instant, she was back in Operation-Night-Stalker mode. *Who could it be?* She pressed herself against the wall – keeping a careful eye out for vases – and crept towards the noise. There was a door slightly ajar, so Ivy peered in through the crack.

Tessa, the maid, was sitting on a stool, crying softly. Ivy remembered how short the Queen had been with her.

'Tessa, are you –' Ivy's words dried up as a strong hand clamped down on her shoulder. She whirled around. 'Horatio!' she gasped. He looked frightening in the night-time gloom.

'You should not skulk in the dark, Miss Ivy,' he said. 'You might scare me.' He chuckled.

'Me? Scare *you*?' Ivy said, her heart still racing.

He began to walk her back towards the staircase and Ivy glanced back over her shoulder at the door Tessa was behind, hoping she would be OK.

'Your father did once,' he admitted. 'He and his brothers always try one trick or another. Little Karl . . . Charles . . . was most ingenious. One night, he hid behind armour and played tape-recorded sounds of dogs barking. When I fled, he followed, playing other sounds like scratching and growling.' The giant butler shook his head. 'I do not like dogs.'

Ivy smiled.

'Happy times,' Horatio said.

Ivy touched him on his gigantic forearm. 'It will be happy times again.'

Horatio nodded. 'Now, it is well past casket-time. You should be sleeping.'

Ivy gave him a quick hug and began the long climb up to her bedroom.

As she crept back into her coffin, Ivy

wondered why poor Tessa had been crying all by herself. *I'll talk to her tomorrow*, she vowed. She knew what it was like to feel lonely and unhappy.

Olivia watched out of the car window for any sign of the palace. It had snowed overnight and there was a coating of white over everything.

'This is quite an honour,' the Countess said. She sat in the front seat of the luxurious eight-seater car, wearing a high-collared ebony jacket over her embroidered dress and short black gloves.

Olivia had chosen her light pink turtleneck and floor-length grey skirt with a wide grey belt and hoped she wasn't under-dressed. Her blue pea coat was on the seat next to her, in case they were outside at all.

'Yes!' came an exclamation from Ivy, who was sitting beside her in her black sweater, pinstripe fitted skirt and multi-buckle boots. She was frantically pressing buttons on her phone. 'Cell-phone signal!'

Olivia's new phone buzzed in her bag. There were two texts from her mom, which she sent a quick reply to, explaining that there wasn't a good signal at the house, and a third text from Jackson. It just said, 'See ya.'

She re-read it seven times.

What does that mean?

Did he send that before she left? Was it a friendly goodbye? Or was it some horribly casual way of breaking it off? It seemed cryptic. No smiley faces, no 'Love, Jackson'. Olivia rubbed her forehead, feeling a headache coming on.

What if she didn't see him soon? She didn't even know what town he was going to next. She wanted to ask Ivy about it, but she couldn't in a car full of adults.

The first chance she had, she would talk to

Ivy about this. Her twin would know what to do. She went back to gazing at the Transylvanian countryside as it sped past the car. Dark, forbidding forests and heavy grey skies. It was so unfamiliar and just made her think how Jackson was thousands of miles away.

'Holy Water!' Ivy whispered to Olivia.

As they drove up the semi-circular gravel driveway, Ivy realised that the Queen's estate made her grandparents' house look like a shed. The two of them peered up at the sculptures of eagles with their wings spread, perched on the top of the stone turret above the entrance.

'It's incredible,' Olivia whispered back, but she wasn't really looking. Ivy wondered if her sister's mind was somewhere else.

Horatio pulled to a stop and climbed out to open the car door. Ivy emerged to see four uniformed staff waiting at the ornate iron doors to greet them.

As she stepped out of the cold wind into the grand entrance, there was no sign of the royal family, but an older woman was calling out to a man who was adjusting light kits and reflectors at the bottom of a sweeping gilded staircase.

'Perfect, daaahling!' she said and swept her floor-length blue coat behind her. The golden flower embroidery on it flashed in the light. Her stark white curls were tamed by a wide clip with an enormous blue and green peacock feather.

Ivy knew that incredible style. 'Georgia Huntingdon!' she said.

The woman whirled around and her blood-red lips split into a wide smile.

'Ivy, darling!' She floated over and air-kissed her on both cheeks. 'And Olivia!'

Olivia looked startled to see the editor of *VAMP* magazine.

'As soon as I heard you two were in Transylvania, connecting with your noble roots,' Georgia purred, 'I simply *had* to capture the event.'

'And we were happy to let her,' the Countess said, air-kissing Georgia.

Mr Vega cleared his throat. 'I wish you had consulted me first, Mother,' he said quietly.

The Countess looked horrified to have upset her son. 'Oh, darling, I –'

But she was interrupted by a voice from the top of the red-carpeted staircase.

'I thought the palace would be the perfect backdrop for a photo shoot,' said Prince Alex, who was watching them from above. He bowed to his guests before stepping lightly down the stairs. He wore a black suit jacket over a white

T-shirt and jeans – he somehow looked modern and classical at the same time.

Ivy realised that everyone else had dropped into a little curtsy or bow and she hurriedly followed suit.

As usual, one step behind, Ivy thought. *At least Georgia is familiar, like a little piece of home.*

'Welcome to the palace,' Alex said to everyone, his glance lingering on Olivia.

Olivia curtsied again. 'It's an honour.'

'The honour is mine,' he said and reached out to kiss her hand.

Georgia leaned in to Ivy. 'Looks like your sister has herself a royal admirer!'

The realisation hit Ivy like a stake in the gut. *Alex likes Olivia!* A second thought followed almost as quickly. *But Olivia has a boyfriend.*

Alex started pointing out features of the gardens at the back of the house, framed by enormous windows. He kept looking at Olivia intensely.

'Oh yes,' she said, 'how pretty.' Her breath misted on the glass as she gazed out at the garden. She had no idea how closely Alex was staring at her.

Georgia clapped her hands and three assistants with racks of clothing hurried out from a side room. 'This feature is going to be even bigger than your first! I simply must have you on the cover of *VAMP* again.'

'Oooh, costumes!' Ivy breathed, wanting to grab a rack and run away with it. Georgia had fabulous taste.

'Of course, this rack is all in your size.' Georgia winked.

'Ivy.' Mr Vega motioned her over. 'Are you OK with all of this?'

'Are you kidding?' Ivy replied. 'A chance to

play dress up with the *VAMP* magazine closets? As long as someone nudges me when I'm putting my foot in it – which I know is pretty often – this might be the best part of my trip!'

Mr Vega nodded. 'If at any time you feel uncomfortable and wish to stop, or leave, just say the word. We are not obligated to stay.'

Ivy felt her heart sink. She understood that their dad wanted to protect his daughters, but couldn't he just go with it for once? 'I want to stay,' Ivy said. 'I want you to want to stay, too.'

Mr Vega looked away. 'I am here for you and your sister.'

Ivy sighed. That wasn't the answer she was hoping for.

Georgia called, 'We'll save the dresses for later, girls. First, I thought we would start with a group photo on the stairs? We'll just wait for Her Majesty –' The older woman suddenly stopped mid-sentence and dropped into an elegant curtsy.

Ivy turned to see the Queen walking down the hallway with two attendants. She was wearing a long-sleeved navy-blue fitted dress with lace detail at the open neck. She looked just as intimidating as she had in her formal gown.

'Welcome,' she said and nodded to the twins. 'Please enjoy your time in my home.' She turned to the magazine editor. 'Shall we?'

Georgia immediately began gently coaxing the Count and Countess up the steps.

'Wouldn't Prince Alex and Olivia look good standing next to each other?' the Countess suggested.

Alex moved instantly to Olivia's side. 'A fabulous idea,' he said.

The Queen raised an eyebrow and Ivy could tell she did not like how much attention her son was paying to the only human in the room.

'No, no,' Mr Vega was saying. 'I don't need to be in the photo.'

'Please, Charles,' Georgia said. 'This is a celebration of togetherness.'

Ivy realised what she was saying: as much as anything could, being in a photo with the Queen was a chance to show the vampire community that times were changing.

'Come on, Dad,' she said. 'You can stand next to me.' She grabbed his arm and pulled him up on to the third step.

As the photographer moved around the group, holding up a light-capture device in front of everyone's faces, Georgia asked, 'Ivy, Olivia, tell me, how are you finding Transylvania? Do you feel like you've come "home"?'

Ivy bit her lip. She wasn't about to let slip how out of place she felt.

Luckily, Olivia came to her rescue. 'We love

Transylvania so far; and everyone here is very nice. Of course, we want to thank Her Majesty and the prince for their gracious hospitality.'

Ivy spotted that Olivia had side-stepped the home question neatly and wondered if anyone else noticed.

Georgia nodded and then turned to the Queen. 'Your Majesty, may I ask what it feels like to open your house to a human for the first time ever?'

The Queen's ruby earrings clinked as she tilted her head. 'It is unusual, to say the least, but this is a *very* special circumstance,' she replied. She nodded at the twins' grandparents. 'The Count and Countess are my closest friends.'

It was a very diplomatic answer, but Ivy sensed she was also saying that she wasn't going to make a habit of inviting non-vamps into her circle. There were plenty of vampires who felt very strongly that vampires and humans shouldn't mix – her own grandparents had made that clear to her father, all those years ago. But the Count and Countess had been nothing but loving to Olivia since she arrived.

'I think,' Prince Alex put in, 'that it shows how well the monarchy is coming to grips with the modern world. I, for one, look forward to these special circumstances becoming more regular.'

The Queen's earrings clinked again as she sat up straighter and drew in a breath.

Two people and one row down, the Count said, 'Times certainly are changing.'

Mr Vega cleared his throat. 'But not everyone wishes to change with them.'

Ivy wanted to say something to cut through all the tension, but the photographer called out, 'We're ready.'

'Smile, my dears,' said Georgia, clasping her hands in front of her chest.

'Stakes!' called the photographer.

'Stakes!' everyone cheered back.

But Ivy suspected that underneath the smiles, conflict was brewing like a bad potion.

❤   ❤   ❤

Olivia was exhausted but happy. She'd worn eight phenomenal dresses, from an Elizabethan-style full-skirted dress to a sleek, asymmetrical gown. Ivy had loved being dressed up and, for once, didn't mind being the centre of attention.

The adults had left at least an hour ago for coffee in the 'presence chamber' as they called it, while Ivy, Olivia and Prince Alex had posed in various luxurious rooms all over the palace.

The Grand Ballroom was truly grand. The windows stretched from floor to ceiling and six crystal chandeliers twinkled over the dance floor. Georgia had wanted them to take turns dancing with Alex – but Ivy had two left feet when it came to ballroom dancing. Olivia was so good at remembering the moves; it turned out to be a photo shoot of the two of them.

Finally, she had the twins pose, one on either side of the prince, in their ball gowns.

'That's the one,' Georgia said, clapping her hands as the photographer finished. 'Next week's cover! I'm going to go look through these on the computer; just hang the dresses up, girls, and I'll send someone back for them.'

'Um, Georgia?' Ivy asked.

'Yes, darling?' she replied.

'Could I borrow this dress for the Valentine's Day ball please?' Ivy knew that she had nothing suitable to wear, and all these dresses had been so wonderful . . .

Georgia considered for a moment. 'No, no, I don't think so.'

'Oh,' Ivy replied, feeling deflated.

'Because I've something better.' She whispered in an assistant's ear and left the room. A moment later, she returned with a big garment bag.

'Wear this.' She winked at Ivy and then produced a pair of Victorian-style lace-up boots. 'With these, and have a faaabulous time.'

'Thank you so much!' Ivy said and started to unzip the bag.

'Ah, ah, ah!' Georgia said. 'Don't spoil the surprise. No peeking until the night of the ball.' She turned to Olivia. 'Would you like a dress as well?'

'I was a little more . . . thorough . . . with my packing,' Olivia replied with a teasing smile at Ivy.

'Then I say: ciao, my lovelies!' Georgia gave a little wave and hurried away, chattering with the photographer.

As Ivy went behind a screen to change, Olivia sat happily on a chair, her silver lace dress spilling over the floor around her.

Alex came to stand beside her. 'Would you do me the honour of accompanying me on a tour of the castle grounds?'

'I'd love to,' Olivia replied. 'We don't have places like this in Franklin Grove. Probably not *anywhere* in America!'

'Wonderful,' Alex said. 'I'll find us some snow boots and be back momentarily.'

As soon as he had left, Ivy poked her head out from behind the screen. 'What are you doing?' she hissed.

Olivia struggled to stand up without damaging the dress and held up the skirt as she walked over to her sister. 'What do you mean?'

'I mean,' Ivy said, zipping up her skirt, 'have you broken up with Jackson and not told me?'

'No,' Olivia replied. 'Although Jackson might have broken up with me.' Olivia felt her headache from the car ride coming back. 'He sent me this weird text message that just said "See ya". And I haven't been able to get a signal again to see if he's sent anything else. What if that's Hollywood speak for, "I want to dump you but am so busy I have to do it by a two-word text"?'

Ivy gave her a don't-be-silly look. 'Your taste in guys is much better than that. You'd never choose one that would do something like that.'

Olivia sighed and turned to let Ivy pull down the zip on her dress. Then she quickly threw on her pink turtleneck. Her mind flashed to Alex. 'But even if Jackson and I are going through a bumpy patch,' Olivia said as she sat back down on the chair to put her tights on, 'Alex and I are just friends.'

'Be careful, Olivia,' Ivy replied. 'His mom is acting so sniffy because she thinks he likes you.'

'A vampire prince wouldn't date a human,' Olivia pointed out.

'You can't say that,' Ivy countered. 'Since you were initiated, most vampires have accepted you. Like the Count said: times are changing.'

Olivia had too much to think about at the moment with Jackson. She couldn't deal with this, too. Besides, there wasn't any spark between her and Alex.

It's not a problem, Olivia decided. *I'm sure of it.*

Just then, Prince Alex returned with two pairs of muddy leather snow boots.

'Milady.' He bowed and held out his arm for her to take. 'Shall we?'

Olivia giggled at his pretend formality and nodded. 'We shall.'

🦇   🦇   🦇

Crunching through the snow and looking up at the tree branches, Olivia thought the royal garden was like a winter wonderland.

She stepped carefully along the slippery stone path. The frosty wind wasn't helping.

'Up here,' Alex said and began climbing a narrow path ascending a hill. Olivia had no choice but to take his arm.

'There is a legend about this hill,' he said when they were about halfway up and Olivia was running out of breath. 'A princess was being forced to marry a man she did not love, to marry for money.' Alex paused in his climb and looked at her sadly. 'On the night before her wedding, she fled the palace and climbed to the top of a tree on this very spot. She hid there all night, crying. When the sun rose and her parents came into the garden, shouting for her to come and be married, she flung herself from the highest branch and died. They say this hill grew from her tears.' Alex turned away and kept walking up the hill.

Some parts of being royalty must be awful, Olivia thought. *Having to marry someone you don't love.*

'Is it still like that?' she asked gently. 'Will *you* have to marry someone your mother chooses?'

Alex's face darkened. 'My mother tends to get her way.'

Olivia gulped. She remembered the Queen's tone with poor Tessa during last night's dinner. She certainly did know how to get what she wanted.

At last, they reached the top of the snowy hill and Olivia caught her breath.

There were mountains on three sides, beautiful peaks, covered in white. Pockets of tiny villages nestled among the trees, their red roofs poking up through the snow.

'It's so beautiful,' Olivia whispered. 'You know, I was worried that I would only feel out of place here. But somewhere inside of me knows that I belong.'

'I'm glad. Look over there.' Alex pointed to a picturesque frozen lake twinkling in the bright winter sun. 'That lake is on your grand-parents' land.'

Olivia looked from the lake to the tops of the stone mansion that she could see through some trees. Her family's estate was enormous.

'And the reason I wanted to show it to you now is because of the poem I mentioned: "Thirteen Ways of Looking at a Blackbird",' Alex went on. 'In the summer, blackbirds thrive around that lake, singing their love songs for all to hear.'

He took a breath. 'The poem is an intense study of one thing, analysing it from every angle – almost obsessed over.'

'I know the feeling,' Olivia said. She hadn't been able to stop thinking about Jackson. She didn't know what to think any more. Right here on this beautiful mountain top was the type of Valentine's Day she'd wanted with Jackson – not waiting in line for a paltry two minutes with him.

She sighed.

'I think the poet wanted to show that you can't judge something, or someone, at first glance.' Alex took her gloved hands in his. 'There is so much to see beyond that.'

It was quiet for a moment. Was the prince trying to tell her something? All this talk of poetry and meanings . . . *It's like we're talking in code*, Olivia thought.

Then Alex grinned. 'But right now, all I can see is a fireplace and a hot drink!'

Olivia chuckled. 'It is *really* cold and a hot

chocolate sounds perfect.'

As they started to walk back down the hill, Olivia wondered, *What if Jackson has started to see me differently? Maybe that explains why he doesn't seem to care any more.*

Ivy sat next to her father on a plush white sofa, not daring to touch the drink that a maid had placed on the glass side table.

Cranberry juice plus white silk fabric equals utter humiliation, Ivy thought, keeping her hands firmly in her lap. There was a delicate glass bowl on the coffee table that could spell disaster as well.

The Queen was sitting across from her, stroking a small white ferret, while her grand-parents sat together on a couch to her right.

'And you shop in the basement of this . . . Food Mart?' The Queen had been asking about Franklin Grove for at least twenty minutes.

'Indeed,' Mr Vega replied. 'Our community thrives alongside the human community, in harmony but in secret.'

'Mmm,' the Queen said. 'It does seem rather . . . unrefined.'

Ivy was glad that she hadn't had to grow up always worrying what the 'refined' thing to do was.

'We have a happy life among humans,' Mr Vega said. 'Many vampires do.'

'My understanding is that you had your own doubts on this matter,' the Queen challenged.

Mr Vega coughed. 'It is true that I thought once that vampires and humans together could only bring harm; I was proven incorrect. Of course humans and vampires can live together happily. My daughters are proof of that.'

Ivy got the sense that the Queen would not tolerate Alex having similar thoughts, despite the fact that he was at this moment escorting Olivia on a private tour of the palace grounds.

'Do tell me the story, Charles,' the Queen commanded. 'Your parents have spent years talking about it in your absence.'

Mr Vega glanced at his mother, but said nothing. Ivy wondered if one of the windows had been left open, as cold air seemed to chill the room.

'Ivy, my dear,' Mr Vega said, 'you must be eager to join your sister exploring the delights of the palace gardens.'

Ivy didn't need asking twice. She nodded and leaped up, almost knocking into the glass bowl, grateful that her father was giving her an excuse to leave – especially because she didn't trust herself to keep her mouth shut if the Queen was dismissive of her parents' story.

She dropped an awkward curtsy and hurried out of the door.

In a hallway lined with tapestries of wolves hunting, Ivy asked a maid where the cloakroom was. She pulled on her crushed velvet coat and headed out into the cold. She could see the footprints where Alex and Olivia had been, and wondered if she would be able to catch them up.

Ten minutes later, Ivy was regretting it. 'This hill is impossible!' she said as the freezing wind whipped her hair into her face.

Two steps after taking a left fork in the path, her foot hit a slick patch of ice and caused her to do the splits. Good thing she was flexible enough not to feel like she'd been ripped in half.

As she picked herself up, she heard a male voice above her. She was almost at the top and realised she could hear Alex speaking, but couldn't quite catch the words.

The voice was coming from a direction that took Ivy slightly off the path. She stepped on

Love Bites

to some stones that led up the hill in a natural staircase.

She poked her head over the crest of the hill and saw her sister talking to the prince by a tree. She could just make out what Alex was saying.

'. . . I think the poet wanted to show that you can't judge something, or someone, at first glance.'

Oh my darkness, Ivy thought. *He's talking about* poetry!

Then Alex grabbed her sister's hands but a gust of wind prevented Ivy from hearing what he said next. *Uh-oh*, she thought. *Picturesque views, clutching hands, poetry, Olivia looking wistful.* Ivy knew exactly what was going on here. It was the day before Valentine's Day and Alex was milking the romance for all it was worth. *The vampire prince has fallen in love with Olivia!*

136

Just then, her foot slipped. She tried to catch herself, flailing her arms and staggering, but it was too late. She twisted over, landed on her backside and slid down half the hill, right into the bushes. A pile of snow fell on top of her.

Ivy wiped chunks of ice from her face. *I should have asked for snow boots!*

She climbed to her feet, brushing the snow off her sleeves.

'So much for my vampire skills,' she muttered. Vampires were meant to be extra-specially agile, but that hadn't stopped her from falling on her behind.

Back to the warm, she decided, marching towards the palace doors. And after that? She'd find out once and for all what the prince was up to.

Chapter Six

'Welcome back, Miss Ivy,' said Horatio as he opened the car door. Ivy breathed a sigh of relief.

Compared to the Queen's estate, this is almost as 'at-home' as the Meat and Greet, Ivy thought.

'Right over there,' Prince Alex was saying to Olivia. He leaned in close to show her where he was pointing.

'That fountain was where I broke my arm, trying to prove to Tessa that I could balance as well as she could,' Alex said. 'I couldn't.' Alex had insisted on accompanying them home.

'I remember that,' the Count said. 'We had to

send you off home in an ambulance. You were only eight.'

Alex smiled at the memory. 'I got into lots of trouble.'

Ivy watched carefully, trying to see if Olivia had realised that Alex seemed to be into her, but Olivia was as relaxed and happy as ever.

Lunch at the palace had involved even smaller portions than last night's dinner so Ivy decided to sneak off to the kitchen for the half hour before they were going to meet in the games room for a darts tournament.

Ivy pulled open the kitchen door and saw Tessa. She was washing plates in the deep ceramic sink. 'Good afternoon, miss,' she said and curtsied, her hands full of soap suds. Strands of dark hair had come out of her long braid, framing her pretty, heart-shaped face.

Ivy felt guilty for interrupting her work. 'No,

no, please, don't be so formal,' Ivy insisted. 'I'm just sneaking in for a snack.'

'Of course, what would you like?' Tessa replied.

'I can make it myself,' Ivy said. 'Please don't stop what you were doing.'

Tessa smiled so that the freckles on her cheeks crinkled up. 'Honestly, I'm happy to do it, and I know where everything is,' she pointed out.

Ivy couldn't argue with that, and she was pleased to see that Tessa had recovered from her crying fit last night. 'OK, you can help, but you aren't allowed to laugh when I put my smiley face of honey on my Platelet Porridge.'

Tessa grinned. 'The Countess does that, too.'

Ivy was glad to learn that there was a fun streak to her grandmother.

'Have you always worked here?' Ivy asked. She

didn't know how to ask Tessa about the crying; she didn't want to embarrass her.

'My father was Horatio's right-hand man before he passed away five years ago, when I was eleven. I grew up here,' Tessa explained, reaching for a saucepan. 'I've only been working since I turned sixteen.'

As Ivy pulled down the box of porridge, Tessa started to speak: 'Er, excuse me, miss. If you don't mind my asking, is everything OK for you? I mean, you've seemed a little upset since you arrived.'

Ivy looked at Tessa, wide-eyed. *But you were crying the other night!* she wanted to say. Still, if Tessa wanted to pretend that had never happened, Ivy would just have to go with it.

'It's been hard to adjust,' she stuttered. 'Especially when my sister fits right in. Everyone loves her – even Prince Alex.'

Tessa stopped stirring the milk into the porridge. 'What do you mean?'

'Olivia's the human. I'm the vampire,' Ivy explained.

'No, I mean, about Prince Alex,' Tessa asked.

'Oh. That he seems interested in Olivia.' When Tessa blinked in confusion, Ivy said, 'You know – romantically.'

'He's not,' Tessa stated.

Ivy put down the honey. 'But I heard him spouting poetry on the hilltop at the palace.'

'I've known him my whole life. He's like that,' Tessa said, turning back to the stove. 'He's just trying to irritate his mother as much as he can. Trust me.'

A warning sign flashed in Ivy's mind. 'What makes you say that?'

'Over the past year, Prince Alex seems to take every opportunity to annoy her.' Tessa shook her head, and put Ivy's bowl of piping hot Platelet Porridge on to the counter. 'Flirting with a human girl will certainly do that. The Queen would burst into fog if the heir to her throne was in a romance with a non-vampire – or anyone she deemed . . . unworthy.'

Ivy felt her blood boil. *Could the prince be pretending? Is he just using Olivia? Well, no boy is going to hurt my sister! I don't care if he's a movie star or a prince!*

But before Ivy could ask for any more details, the kitchen door was flung open and Olivia burst in.

'There you are!' she said. 'Come on! Alex and I want to go to the frozen lake to ice-skate. I already asked the Countess, and she said we can borrow whatever we want.'

'There are plenty of pairs of ice skates in the shed,' said Tessa.

Love Bites

'What about playing darts inside where it's *warm*?' Ivy said, wanting to avoid anything that involved her sliding around on ice. Her behind was still throbbing from that fall outside the palace.

'Oh, I've already proven that I can beat Alex hands down,' Olivia said, grabbing an apple out of the fruit bowl. 'Let's skate! Tessa, will you join us?'

Ivy wanted to say something about Alex, but the last time she'd become involved in Olivia's love life, she'd made a mess of things. She sighed. *I'll have to wait until I'm absolutely O-positive that Prince Alex is up to no good.*

'Come on, Ivy!' Olivia was bouncing on the spot. 'Tessa is coming.'

This could be a chance to watch Alex with Olivia, Ivy thought. *I can see what he's trying to do.*

'OK,' she said, 'I'll come, but not until I've eaten my porridge.'

144

Wow, these Transylvanians are good, Olivia thought as she skated along steadily.

A few of the prince's friends had arrived on the frozen lake, joining Olivia, Ivy, Alex, Tessa and Nadia, the other young maid. A blond guy with a buzz cut was skating backwards in sync with a red-headed girl, both with one leg out in an arabesque. Another two girls were practising spins in the middle. One of them had her black hair slicked back in a high, long ponytail and her dark silver coat looked almost metallic. Her friend had on a black-and-white patterned coat and a black beret. They looked like Olympic gold medallists who had skated right off the catwalk.

Except, Olivia thought, *it would be cheating if they actually competed in the Olympics because of the whole vampire super powers thing.*

'Come on, Olivia!' called Alex. 'Show us what you can do!'

Olivia smiled and looked at the red-headed girl, who was now doing a fast spin. 'I can't compete with that!'

She sped up a little bit and let Alex take her arms to push her even faster. Olivia hadn't ice-stated much, but her cheerleader's balance and grace helped her to at least keep up with the vampires.

As they sped across the ice together into the wind, the white of the snow, the brown of the trees and the blue of the sky smeared across her vision. It was another moment that she wished Jackson could have been a part of.

Jackson, Olivia thought. *I've got to tell Alex.* Ivy's warnings had spooked her; it was best that she explain to the prince about her boyfriend back home. But just when she was about to say

146

something, Ivy skated over with Tessa.

Or Tessa skated and Ivy sort of shuffled and fell forwards, clutching Tessa's arm. Tessa was wearing a cosy-looking, well-loved wool coat with big black buttons.

'I thought you vampires were supposed to be good at all things athletic,' Olivia teased Ivy.

Tessa grinned. 'It's not her body; it's her mind. She's got the Fear.'

'After my episode in the mall, and a little slip earlier today –' Ivy grimaced – 'I don't want to fall on my already sore butt.'

Olivia chuckled but Alex didn't seem to be listening.

'Hello . . . Your Highness,' Tessa said.

'Uh, h-hello, Tessa,' he said. Olivia was surprised to hear Alex stutter. It sounded as though he was going to say something else but was holding back. He offered a quick nod that was almost a bow. 'Excuse me.' Then he skated away towards his friends.

'I should go, too,' said Tessa. 'I'll get back to the kitchen.'

Why is everyone leaving? Olivia wondered.

Ivy frowned and called after Tessa, 'Don't go!' But she was already zooming away.

'Alex was so rude to Tessa just then,' Ivy declared and started awkwardly skating after Tessa towards the edge of the lake.

Olivia hadn't noticed. 'What? How was he rude? No, I'm sure he didn't mean anything.' When Ivy wobbled she held out her hand for her sister to hold on to.

Ivy shot a look over at Alex and his friends.

The girl with the slick ponytail was sniggering. 'And did you see her ancient coat?' they overheard the girl say.

'See?' Ivy hissed. 'Alex and his friends don't

want to be around Tessa because she's a servant.'

'That's too harsh,' Olivia replied, as they neared the frozen mud and grass that surrounded the lake. 'Alex didn't say anything bad about her. He probably just wants to spend time with everyone equally.'

Ivy almost collapsed on to the ground and started unlacing her boots. 'You saw how his mother acted towards Tessa last night at dinner.'

Olivia looked back at the group, laughing and playing tag. It definitely wasn't OK with her if they were being mean to someone just because of their job.

'And are you sure *you* should be spending this much time with Alex?' Ivy asked.

'I don't know,' Olivia replied. She didn't want to think that her friendship with Alex might be wrong in some way.

Ivy narrowed her eyes. 'Well, do what feels

right. Don't let me stop you from enjoying the skating.' Ivy waved her sister away and back on to the ice. 'I'll wait here.'

Olivia hesitated. 'You sure?' she asked.

Ivy patted the log she was sitting on. 'Firm ground and me, we're good friends. Besides, how often do you get to skate on a frozen lake?'

Olivia pushed off and skated smoothly round in a big loop. When she looked back over her shoulder, Ivy was watching her intently.

When Olivia turned back to where she was going, she just had time to realise she was skating straight towards Nadia, the younger maid. There was no time to change direction!

'Move out of the way, quick!' Olivia shrieked, waving her arms madly. But it was too late. She and Nadia crashed into each other.

Olivia landed on her backside while Nadia ended up on her front.

'Oh my goodness,' Olivia said, scrambling up to make sure Nadia was all right. 'I'm so sorry!'

'Don't worry, miss,' she replied. 'I'm fine – oh!' Her hands flew to her neck. 'My necklace!'

Olivia scanned the ground and saw a gold chain, broken at the clasp, lying on the ice. She held up the necklace to get a closer look and was relieved to see that the clasp was just bent out of shape. 'I can fix this,' she declared.

'Olivia!' Alex called. 'Come over here with us.'

Olivia wanted to, but she'd practically just tackled poor Nadia. She shook her head and called back, 'I can't, not now.'

Alex frowned but Olivia turned back to Nadia and helped her up. 'Come with me and we'll get this fixed,' she said.

She skated Nadia over to the edge of the lake. Ivy was watching Alex with a scowl as she held her arm out for Olivia to hold on to. 'That had to hurt,' said Ivy. 'I wonder if we'll have twin bruises.'

Olivia rubbed her rear. 'I'd rather not know,' she joked.

Ice-skating on the lake was supposed to be fun, but instead it had turned into a slippery situation with Alex and Ivy and Tessa – and poor Nadia.

Plus, she *still* hadn't managed to tell Alex about Jackson.

🦇　　🦇　　🦇

An hour later, Ivy didn't recognise herself.

She was wearing a pink shirt with frilled sleeves, a knee-length white skirt, white woolly boots and a good layer of Santa Monica Sun in a Bottle on her face. The shirt wasn't Olivia's most flattering – the frills looked like jellyfish blobs – but it was pink so it would do.

There was one final touch she couldn't go

without. She picked up Olivia's Blush and Bashful lip gloss, took a deep breath and applied it.

This could get me into batloads of trouble, Ivy thought, *but I need to know what Prince Alex is up to.*

The idea had come to her as she was watching Olivia and Alex on the ice. She had to find out Alex's motives. *I can't do that as Ivy.* Alex barely seemed to notice that she existed. *But as Olivia?* She could find out a whole lot of information.

And when Olivia had rushed off with Nadia, Ivy knew it was now or never.

She practised a hair flip in the mirror, careful not to knock the feathery pink hairband. *Yup, still got it.*

Olivia was busy fixing Nadia's necklace in the servants' quarters and Ivy knew that Alex had already come back from the lake.

As long as I don't run into Olivia, I'll be fine, Ivy thought.

She started trudging down the steps to the ground floor, but then realised who she was supposed to be. She forced a little spring into her step and bounced the rest of the way.

Being Olivia takes a lot more energy than being me.

At the bottom of the stairs, Horatio was waiting, like he knew she was coming.

'Horatio!' Ivy said, glad she'd decided to perk up on her way down. 'Have you seen the prince anywhere?'

Horatio frowned and peered at her, like he could sense something was wrong. Ivy guessed she had about three seconds before her cover was blown. Ivy did the only thing she could think of to do: she flipped her long brown hair.

'I last saw him heading towards the kitchen, Miss Olivia,' Horatio said and bowed.

'Thanks!' Ivy said and squeezed past him.

She hurried into the hallway, looking around

for anyone but seeing only the landscape paintings of the Carpathian mountains on the walls.

Pausing at the kitchen door and taking a deep breath, Ivy told herself, *Think pink, think perky*. She put her hand up to push open the kitchen door, but it swung open before she even touched it.

Ivy looked at her hand. *Did I do that?* She wondered if she'd manifested some crazy new vampire power, but then Prince Alex stepped through, leaving the kitchen.

Ivy just caught a glimpse of Tessa leaning against the counter with tears streaming down her cheeks. Alex's mouth was set in a scowl, which turned to a smile when he saw Ivy – well, when he saw 'Olivia'.

'Hi!' Ivy said as brightly as she could, but really wanted to shout, *What have you done to poor Tessa, you big, mean snob!*

Even if he wasn't trying to use her sister, Ivy didn't want Olivia being friends with someone who made servants cry.

'Hello, Olivia,' Alex said, hastily shutting the door behind him and offering his arm. 'Just the person I wanted to see.'

Ivy plastered on her biggest, bunniest smile and hooked her arm through his. 'I was looking for you, too,' she said.

Operation Royal Reveal has begun.

'There is a book that I want to show you,' he explained as he led her along the corridor, looking nervously over his shoulder back towards the kitchen. 'Come with me.' He was virtually dragging Ivy along now, and she gently freed her arm from his.

'Lead the way!' she said.

He pushed open a door to a room that Ivy hadn't been in yet. It was a dimly lit, cosy library with wood panelling, red leather chairs and books from floor to ceiling. She breathed deeply, taking in the smell of leather and dust.

Ivy touched the dark wood of the ladder that was attached to a railing high above her head. 'This room is beautiful,' she said.

'It is, isn't it? As a child, your family would allow me to come and read in here on visits.' Alex was peering intently at one of the shelves at eye-level.

'That's it!' he declared and pulled out a tall, green leather-bound book. The title was pressed into the leather in gold – *Legends of the Lazar* – and there was an ornate outline of a leafy tree.

Alex placed the book on a wooden book stand and opened it.

'This is the oldest known version of the story I told you about, the princess in the tree.' Alex pointed to a page of calligraphy with an intricate big letter with vine leaves twirling around it to begin the story.

'Oh, yes,' Ivy said faintly. What story? Was he talking about the poem she'd heard him reciting to Olivia on the hill? She'd just have to pretend that she knew what he was talking about.

The story was in Romanian, so Ivy couldn't read it, but the image on the opposite page was of a beautiful girl wearing flowing robes and a crown. It was enough for Ivy to guess what Alex liked about the story: a beautiful princess is rescued by a handsome prince and lives happily ever after, bossing around servants and lording it over everyone for the rest of their lives.

No more Miss Nice Olivia, Ivy thought. *Time to get down to business.*

'So, Alex,' Ivy said, putting on her cheeriest voice. 'Tell me about your mother.'

Alex looked a little like a sleeping fawn that

had just had a torch shined in its face: startled and about to flee.

❤   ❤   ❤

'Good as new,' Olivia declared, holding up the necklace so that Nadia could see it was fixed. Nadia had taken her to the servants' quarters on the second floor, where she'd used pliers from the toolbox.

'Miss Olivia, you are too kind,' Nadia replied, putting the chain back around her neck. 'You didn't have to do that.'

'It was the least I could do,' Olivia replied. 'And please, just call me Olivia. No "Miss".'

Nadia nodded. 'OK . . . Olivia.' Then she blushed a little.

As Olivia stood up to go, she caught sight of a Romanian magazine with Jackson on the cover. Her stomach clenched. She remembered her first day filming on the movie set. Jackson had arranged for a playlist of all her favourite songs to be playing in her trailer while she was getting ready. *He* can *be romantic and sweet,* she thought. *So why isn't he making more of an effort?* She hadn't heard anything else from him. Even if the phone signal was dreadful here, she couldn't help feeling that if Jackson really cared he'd have found out the landline number or something.

'Well, I'm sorry again about clobbering you on the ice,' Olivia said to Nadia.

'That's OK. I should probably get back to work,' Nadia said.

They gave each other a little hug and Olivia left the servants' quarters. Her confusion about Jackson threatened to take over all the good feelings she was having being here with her family.

Ivy will be able to help, Olivia thought. *Find Ivy.*

Down the hallway, Olivia caught sight of

Horatio wiping dust off a frame that no normal-sized person would be able to reach.

'Hey, Horatio,' she said, hurrying over. 'Have you seen Ivy?'

Horatio frowned at her, looking behind him and back. 'Did you spill something, Miss Olivia?'

'Um, no,' she replied, wondering why he would think she had.

'Hmmm.' His fuzzy eyebrows furrowed. 'I have not seen Miss Ivy recently.'

'OK, no problem,' she said. 'If you see her, could you ask her to find me?'

'I shall,' he said and went back to his dusting. As she walked away, Olivia heard him mutter: 'How many twins are there?'

She wandered down the corridors, asking anyone she came across about Ivy, but no one seemed to have seen her. Down one hallway, she heard Prince Alex's deep voice coming from a room. *Maybe he's seen Ivy*, she thought, and headed towards the door.

Chapter Seven

'And I'm sick of her telling me what to do all the time!' Alex was still talking. 'She's a control freak, living her life through me. Doesn't she understand? I need some freedom to make my own decisions!' Alex sounded just like any other teenager complaining about his parents, and for a moment Ivy almost felt sorry for him – almost. But she quickly reminded herself that she was on a mission. *I'll get the truth out of him*, she swore. *One way or another.*

'Which is why I'm so glad that you're here,' Alex finished, giving her a big smile.

Ah ha! Ivy thought. *Because you want to make your mom mad!*

'Because now I have lots of excuses to leave the palace.' Alex sat back in the chair, relaxing.

Ivy adjusted her white skirt and tugged at the pink hairband that was starting to tickle her ears. She pushed away the guilty feeling for impersonating her sister. This was important.

'Would your mom be mad that you were spending time with me?' Ivy asked.

Before he could answer, a panel of books swung open, making Ivy jump. Alex stood up and Ivy watched to see who was coming in with her heart pounding.

Please don't be Olivia, Ivy thought.

It was one of the Queen's footmen, who bowed sharply and said, 'Your Highness, word has been sent from the palace.'

Alex sighed.

'You are to attend your mother immediately,' the footman finished.

Alex looked like he was going to say something but he stopped himself. His body stiffened and Ivy realised that in front of the footman, Alex had slipped back into his role as prince. 'Yes, of course.' He turned to 'Olivia'. 'I'm sorry to leave you so abruptly.' He gave a tense smile, and kissed Ivy's hand. 'Good day, Olivia. I hope to see you again soon.'

Ivy smiled and curtsied. *Just when I was about to get the confession!*

Alex disappeared through the panel behind the footman.

It doesn't matter, Ivy thought. *It's pretty clear from his ranting about being controlled that he is using Olivia to annoy his mother.*

Now all Ivy had to do was get upstairs, de-Olivia-fy herself and then convince her sister that Prince Alex was bad news.

But how?

She pulled open the door and blinked. She'd come face-to-face with someone. It was just like looking in a mirror.

Ivy gasped. 'Olivia!'

'Ivy?' Olivia said.

🦇   🦇   🦇

'I can't believe you!' Olivia stormed up the stairs to their shared bedroom, feeling hurt, confused and really, really un-perky.

'I'm sorry,' Ivy said.

'You've said that,' Olivia snapped.

'If you'll just let me explain –' Ivy began.

Olivia whirled around, two steps above her sister. 'This is the ultimate twin betrayal, Ivy!'

Ivy took a step down with her mouth open.

'Switching without permission? It's like . . . like body-snatching! Identity theft!' Olivia marched into their room, not even holding the door open for Ivy.

'Please, Olivia,' Ivy said, pushing through the doorway.

Olivia struggled to keep her voice even. 'I know you've been having trouble adjusting here but I'd never expect you to do *this*.'

'But —' Ivy was backing away, almost into the big wooden wardrobe.

'Dressing up like me to spend time with Prince Alex is plain devious, Ivy,' Olivia said.

'If you would just stop shouting —'

But Olivia didn't want to hear whatever Ivy had to say. Her own sister had been keeping secrets from her. She never thought *that* would happen.

'Girls?' came the Countess's voice from the doorway, and instantly Olivia regretted yelling. 'Girls, what's the matter?' Their grandmother's glance flickered from Olivia to Ivy, wearing similar outfits, and realisation spread across her face. 'I see.'

Olivia shot a look at Ivy.

'Something has obviously happened between you two, and I don't need details,' the Countess said. 'But you both should know that nothing that ever happens between you stops you being *family*.'

Olivia crossed her arms.

'You are sisters – twins – there is nothing more important than that bond.' She motioned for both of them to come over and give her a hug. Olivia didn't want to refuse her grandmother but she didn't want to be that close to Ivy at the minute, either.

She stubbornly waited for Ivy to go over first.

'You, too, Olivia,' the Countess said.

Olivia shot her sister a Death Squint and hugged her grandmother, making sure she didn't touch Ivy at all.

The Countess pulled back and looked at them both. 'There is nothing that can't be resolved with a good talk. I'm going to leave now, and you are going to stay here until you work out whatever it is that caused all this squabbling.'

Olivia sighed and her grandmother took both her hands.

'Believe me,' she said. 'Fighting with your family is awful.'

Olivia looked into her clear blue eyes and realised that her grandmother was talking about her biological dad. She'd fallen out with her son and it had taken Charles fifteen years to come back here. As the Countess left the room, Olivia imagined if ten years from now she and Ivy weren't talking. *I wouldn't know where she was or what she was doing.*

The thought made her anger fade a little.

Olivia examined her sister. 'I never should have brought that shirt,' she said. 'Those frilly sleeves are horrible.'

Ivy gave a hopeful smile. 'I picked it because I thought it was the most cheerleader thing in your suitcase.'

'Hmph,' Olivia said. 'So . . .'

'So, what?' Ivy asked.

'So why are you dressed up as me and talking to Prince Alex?'

Ivy pulled Olivia over to sit on her coffin. 'OK,' Ivy began. 'I wasn't trying to get closer to Prince Alex. I think he's pretending to be interested in you to get back at his mother. If I pretended to be you, I hoped I could trick him into revealing what he was up to.'

Olivia couldn't believe that Alex would have any ulterior motive. 'But Alex and I are just friends.'

Ivy raised an eyebrow. 'Private tours of

the palace? Poetry on the top of a hill? Taking you ice-skating? That's all pretty romantic for someone who just wants to be friends.'

Olivia had to admit that the walk on the hilltop had been pretty romantic.

Ivy went on. 'And ever since Jackson was all weird about Valentine's Day, you've been brooding over him, so maybe Prince Alex seemed like a better option. But if he's just pretending, I wasn't going to let him break your heart.'

Olivia remembered what he'd said after he recited the poem: something about longing to escape his circle. Had he been trying to tell her something? The Queen had made it pretty clear that she only just tolerated humans in her presence, and Alex could have been saying how his mother would never let him have a human girlfriend.

'You might be right,' Olivia admitted to her

sister. 'Not about him pretending, I don't think, but about him liking me.'

'Do you like him back?' Ivy asked.

Olivia was asking herself the same question. An odd feeling crept over her and she was surprised to hear herself say, 'I don't know.'

Jackson had always seemed perfect for her – except for when she thought he might have been a vampire – and, even though they hadn't kissed yet, being his girlfriend made her so happy . . . usually. Lately, being his girlfriend had been kind of hard. These past two days with Alex had been a breeze by comparison. No long lines of girls, no rushing off anywhere, no Amy Teller hovering over them looking at her watch.

Then something occurred to her.

'Oh dear,' Olivia said aloud.

'What?' Ivy wanted to know.

'He doesn't know I'm dating Jackson,' Olivia

replied. 'I'd tried to tell him when we were ice-skating but couldn't find the right moment.'

'That was worrying me,' Ivy said. 'At least now we know he wasn't ready to ruin your relationship with Jackson in order to get back at his mum. That *would* have made him evil.'

Olivia couldn't imagine Alex being cruel; he seemed so sensitive. 'Are you absolutely sure about this?'

'His mother is a separationist, and everyone says they fight a lot.' Ivy jumped up and started pacing. 'Having a human girlfriend would be one sure-fire way to make his mom really angry.'

Olivia sighed. 'I think you're right that Alex is sometimes unhappy with what his mother and his position demand of him, but he's not a bad person.'

Olivia was worried it was worse than him pretending to like her; what if he really did like her? If that was true, she was going to have to do something about it. She was with Jackson, and even if things were weird between them right now, she had to stay true to him.

'So . . .' Ivy said.

'So, what?' Olivia asked.

Ivy sat back down on the coffin. 'Am I forgiven?'

'You're forgiven,' Olivia replied, giving her sister a big hug. 'As long as we can bury that shirt in my suitcase and forget I ever bought it.'

'Deal,' Ivy said.

'Or maybe I should make you keep wearing it as punishment?' Olivia grinned wickedly.

Ivy let out a strangled noise and hurriedly pulled it off.

The next morning at breakfast, Ivy was delighted to see a table of pancakes, sausages, hash browns and eggs laid out buffet-style.

'Yum,' she said to Olivia as they entered the dining room with their father. He sat down towards the foot of the table. 'Nudge me if I look like a werewolf during a full moon.'

The Countess beamed from her position at the head of the table. 'I'm so glad you like it. It was Tessa's idea.'

Ivy grinned at her new friend, who was laying out a selection of maple syrups, and mouthed, 'Thank you!'

Tessa smiled back. She held up a bottle and made a show of pointing to it and mouthing, 'Try this one.'

'Now, fill up, girls,' the Count said as he sat down opposite his wife. 'Your grandmother will be putting you to work soon with all the preparations for this evening.'

Ivy didn't need telling twice and heaped food

on to her plate. She made sure to choose the maple syrup that Tessa had recommended, which was labelled 'Apricot Maple Syrup'.

The Countess cleared her throat. 'Charles, my son.'

Ivy paused in her feasting, sensing that something was about to happen.

'I had hoped that you would be by my side tonight and escort me into the ball?' The Countess spoke slowly but with a hopeful look on her face. 'Like you used to do?'

Please say yes, Ivy wished. *Please!*

Ivy remembered what he'd said in the car before they'd arrived at the house. He was only here for his daughters – but maybe spending time here had convinced him to forgive his parents?

Mr Vega hesitated. 'I regret to say that I am not feeling entirely myself today and so do not think I will be able to attend. I apologise.'

'Of course,' said the Countess, her voice catching in her throat. 'I hope you feel . . . better . . . soon.'

Ivy didn't know what to say and the rest of breakfast passed in almost silence. Half an hour later, she leaned back in her chair and rubbed her full belly.

'Now you look like a werewolf who *ate* a full moon.' Olivia said, laughing.

'Mmm.' Ivy smiled. 'Bliss.'

'Come along, now, my darlings,' the Countess said, getting to her feet. 'There are a few things to do before the ball tonight.'

Ivy pulled herself out of her chair, gripping the edge of the table.

'Should I get you a crane?' Olivia teased.

'How about one of those motorised scooters?' Ivy replied, trudging after her grandmother into the parlour. Piles of silky red and black ribbons waited for them on each of the polished oak side tables.

'You girls can sit there.' The Countess pointed to a sofa behind one of the tables with ribbon. 'And the gentlemen can share that pile to help me wrap the party gifts.'

Mr Vega followed the Count towards two armchairs and sat down, dutifully.

The Count poked at the ribbon. 'Perhaps I'll leave the pretty bows to you girls,' he said, before settling into a chair and pulling a book out of his jacket. He was soon hidden behind its pages, chuckling at whatever he was reading.

'Mmm, sitting,' Ivy said to Olivia, plopping down heavily.

'I'll get Tessa to bring in the presents.' The Countess called down the hall.

'Presents?' Olivia asked, looking the most excited Ivy had seen her since they'd arrived. The

Countess had come back into the room.

'Last year, we gave everyone a portable music player pre-filled with love songs,' the Countess said.

Ivy and Olivia shared a look. *Wow*, Ivy thought. *They take Valentine's really seriously in Transylvania.*

'And this year . . .' the Countess paused until Tessa appeared in the doorway, carrying a tray of small silver boxes. 'We're giving everyone a visit from my favourite feng shui expert in honour of you two and your father. It's a gift to help everyone find harmony in their home.'

'That's amazing,' said Olivia and Ivy thought so, too.

She snuck a glance at her father. He was neatly sorting the ribbons into tidy rolls, lined up on the table. He didn't seem to have heard a word the countess had said.

'Yes,' his mother repeated, gazing at Mr

Vega. 'A harmonious home is so important for a family.' Ivy could see her dad's cheeks colouring, even as he twirled another piece of ribbon around his finger.

Come on, Dad, she thought. *Can't you just put your differences aside and come to the ball?*

Ivy went over to help Tessa set the tray down on the table. Together, they placed a few stacks of boxes next to each pile of ribbons. She noticed that Tessa's face was pale and she had dark circles beneath her eyes, as though she hadn't been sleeping.

'Are you OK?' Ivy whispered.

Tessa nodded quickly, not making eye contact. 'I'm fine,' she said. Ivy wasn't so sure. Her friend looked . . . unhappy.

'I want us to tie one red and one black ribbon around each box,' the Countess declared.

Olivia picked up one of the little boxes and

Ivy saw her look inside. There was a tiny scroll that unravelled to reveal a stunning calligraphy message. 'These are beautiful,' Olivia said. Party planning was one of her particular skills, and now Ivy had a good idea where she inherited it from.

'Don't tell anyone what's inside,' the Countess said. 'It's my big surprise of the evening.'

'We promise,' Ivy replied. She picked up one red and one black ribbon, but before she could ask how her grandmother wanted it to look, Horatio stepped into the doorway.

'Her Majesty the Queen and the Crown Prince Alexander,' he said and stepped aside.

The Queen swept into the room, wearing a beige dress with tiny hook and eye buttons of matching fabric running down one side and a little matching hat. Prince Alex was wearing a white knitted sweater with dark jeans and was carrying a suit bag over his shoulder.

Tessa kept her eyes on the ground and slipped out of the door behind them.

Ivy quickly dropped the ribbon and stood up to curtsy. She was a split second before Olivia.

Finally getting the hang of it, she thought.

The Queen nodded to everyone and air-kissed the Countess.

Prince Alex bowed formally. 'Countess Lazar,' he said, 'would you mind if I got ready for the ball here? There's little point going all the way back to the palace only to return again this evening.'

The Queen's brow creased in a slight frown, Ivy noticed, but she didn't protest.

'Of course, that's fine.' The Countess motioned for Horatio to take the garment bag. 'Horatio will prepare the third-floor guest suite for you.'

'Thank you,' Alex replied and went to sit across from Olivia.

'I trust I have not missed much.' The Queen

glided over to one of the gold armchairs and sat delicately.

'Only the revelation to my granddaughters of what is in the boxes,' the Countess said. 'Thank you so much for coming to help with our preparations.'

'Not at all.' The Queen leaned forward and started to open a lid.

'Ah, ah.' The Countess batted at the Queen's hand. 'No peeking!'

Ivy was surprised to see the Queen smile. 'I don't know how you're going to exceed last year's party, dear Caterina,' she said. 'But I know it will be the event of the season.'

'With Olivia and Ivy here,' Alex said, 'there's no question.'

The Queen's smile vanished.

'Which is why –' Alex looked straight at Olivia and Ivy guessed what was going to happen next.

'I hope Olivia would not mind preventing me from attending alone.'

Olivia froze. The Countess smiled with delight but the Queen sat stiffly, her back rigid and her gaze straight ahead.

Olivia and Ivy shared a glance. Ivy guessed that the same things were running through her sister's mind: if Olivia said yes, the Queen could be outraged, but if she said no, she could be offending their grandmother's most important guest. On top of everything, Olivia still hadn't told Alex that she had a boyfriend.

Ivy wanted to put a stop to everything – tell Alex to stop trying to annoy his mother, and tell the Queen to stop being so anti-human. But there was nothing Ivy could say that wouldn't get her into enormous trouble.

'Do you think that is appropriate?' said the Queen.

'I certainly can't predict what *you* find appropriate, Mother,' Alex replied.

Mr Vega cut in. 'If it is what they want, then it is entirely appropriate.'

'It is what I want, Mother,' Prince Alex said.

All eyes were on the Queen.

Ivy gulped. *Is this going to turn into a separationist argument?*

The Countess came to the rescue.

'Of course, Prince Alex,' she said. 'Olivia would be delighted to be presented with you, as your new friend.'

'Yes,' Olivia said quickly, and Ivy could see her take a breath. That was just the right thing for the Countess to say. 'Yes, of course. As your new friend.'

Alex beamed and the Queen nodded.

'How lovely,' she said, but there wasn't any hint of warmth in her eyes.

Ivy saw a look on her father's face, astonishment that the Countess seemed happy for Olivia and Alex to spend time together. Maybe he was finally starting to see that his parents had changed.

Just then, Tessa came back into the room, carrying a tray with a pot and cups. 'Tea, Your Majesty?'

The Queen turned her face away, not even bothering to reply. Tessa hesitated there for a moment, unsure what to do.

Alex was still glaring at his mother. 'I'll pour my own tea.' He took the tray from a horrified-looking Tessa and turned his back on her.

How can these people be so rude? Ivy thought. Olivia, too, looked surprised at the behaviour of the Queen and her son. *Refusing to let Tessa pour his tea. Just because Tessa works in the house doesn't make them any better than her.*

It was all bubbling up inside Ivy and she couldn't stop herself. 'How can you –' she began to say. But she caught herself in time. *Don't ruin things.* She quickly turned to Olivia. 'How do you get those bows so straight, Olivia?'

Tessa practically fled as Alex poured his tea and the conversation turned to different methods of tying the ribbons.

Ivy wanted to march right out of the room, pack up her suitcase and go back home. She missed Brendan. She wished she could be back at home, in Franklin Grove, where she belonged.

But I'm not going home yet. I am going to do something! Ivy thought. *I'll stop the way they're treating Tessa.*

🦇　　　🦇　　　🦇

Olivia's brain was on the verge of exploding. Ivy had been pacing ever since they'd returned to their bedroom.

'Why did he have to ask you in front of his

mom?' Ivy was ranting. 'And they were so rude to Tessa!' She was stomping and throwing her hands around. 'What if he really does like you?' She turned and advanced on Olivia. 'It is the *Valentine's Day* ball, Olivia.'

'OK, OK!' Olivia cried. Anything to make her sister stop. 'It's all really complicated.'

There was a knock on the door.

'Girls?' called Mr Vega.

Olivia shot Ivy a panicked look. 'Oh gosh, I hope he didn't hear any of that.' She was getting closer to her biological father, but she didn't want him knowing all about her crazy love life.

'Come in,' Ivy called back.

Mr Vega poked his head inside the room. 'I just wanted to check on you. Your grandmother mentioned that you had a disagreement last night?'

Olivia was relieved to see that he didn't seem to have heard anything. She nodded and motioned for him to come in. 'Yes, we're fine.' She looked over at her sister, who looked a little guilty. 'It was just a misunderstanding.'

'No big deal,' Ivy said, as he sat down on the chair at her dressing table.

'That's good to hear,' Mr Vega replied. 'These things happen – and will probably happen again – so I'm glad you can talk through it.'

Olivia realised the same thing could apply to him.

'What about you?' she asked gently.

Mr Vega blinked.

'I mean, how is it being back?' Olivia had felt the terrible tension in the parlour earlier and hoped that maybe the Countess had done enough to prove that she was trying to make up for the past.

'Some things are like I remember and some things are not,' he replied. 'But I am glad you are both getting along with the family.'

That didn't really answer my question, Olivia thought.

Mr Vega stood up. 'Well, tonight should be something special. Your grandmother always goes to great lengths for this ball – I loved it at your age. Everyone will be there, including Georgia's camera crew.'

As he left, Olivia felt her stomach tighten. *A camera crew*, Mr Vega had said. *That means photographic evidence of me walking into a ball with a handsome young man that isn't Jackson.*

'Ivy, what am I going to do about Alex?' Olivia asked. 'Is it too late to tell him about my boyfriend? I don't want to hurt his feelings.' Olivia took a deep breath. 'I don't want to lose Jackson. Whatever that text meant, I'd like to talk it out with him.'

'I don't know, sis,' Ivy replied.

There was another knock at the door.

'Who is it?' Ivy asked.

'It's me,' called Tessa. 'I . . . have a present.'

'A present?' Olivia pulled open the door.

'It's for you.' Tessa held out a big flat box wrapped in bright red Valentine's Day paper.

'Me?' Olivia squeaked.

'It's just arrived,' Tessa explained.

Olivia took the box and put it on the dressing table.

Tessa curtsied and said, 'If you need any help getting ready for the ball, I'm pretty good with hair.'

'Thanks, Tessa,' Ivy replied. 'We can all get ready in here together.'

Tessa blushed. 'Um, well, I won't need to get ready, as such.'

Olivia realised what she was saying, but Ivy didn't. 'What do you mean?'

'Servants are on duty at the ball,' Tessa explained, 'so we wear uniform.'

Ivy crossed her arms. 'I am so totally done with all this snobbery.'

'Tessa, why do you stay if people are rude to you?' Olivia asked.

'Oh no, they aren't rude. I love working for your grandparents, and Horatio is a big teddy bear.' Tessa sighed. 'It's just the Queen. She . . . doesn't like me much.'

'She is outright rude to you.' Ivy had a determined look in her eye. 'And now I learn you don't even get to celebrate like everyone else at the ball.'

'I don't mind that,' Tessa said. 'That's just how things work.' But Olivia could see that Ivy was shaking her head.

'I hope you will come and help us get ready,' Olivia said. 'And tell us all about what to expect at the ball.'

Tessa brightened. 'Of course!' She curtsied and left.

Olivia turned back to the box. 'Should I open this?'

Ivy stood by her side, watching as she peeled back the shiny red paper. There wasn't a card, but the box carried a prestigious department store logo, with 'Krullers of Transylvania' written in swirly writing beneath it.

'You have to,' Ivy declared.

Olivia drew in a breath and lifted off the lid. Inside was a thick garment bag and a scroll. She unrolled the worn-looking paper to read, 'There is so much I want to say. I'll start with this on Valentine's Day: wear tonight this dress of blue, which shows the way I feel for you.'

The poem wasn't signed, but she knew exactly who it had to be from. 'Prince Alex,' Olivia said, feeling her heart tumble like it was twisting its ankle after a badly executed high kick. She'd wanted a big romantic gesture like this from Jackson, and it being from Alex made everything feel that much worse. How could Jackson have known that she had to wear something special tonight?

'I don't want to see it,' Olivia said.

'Then I'll do it,' Ivy said. 'We have to know how bad this is.'

She took out the dress, still in its black protective bag on its hanger, and hung it up on one of the wardrobe doors.

'Drum roll,' whispered Ivy.

To Olivia, it was a drum roll of doom.

She unzipped the bag and caught a flash of ice-blue silk. Then she pushed away the black plastic and gasped. It was a floor-length slim-line gown with a wide slash neck; simple, with one eye-catching detail: a wide band of ruffled silk at the waist. The hem curved like flower petals and the fabric felt smooth and cool. It was breathtaking.

'Oh my darkness,' Ivy breathed, as Olivia reached out to feel the cool, delicate fabric.

'It's totally gorgeous,' Olivia said, amazed at how well Alex had guessed at her taste and style. 'Whoever bought this has perfect taste.' She looked at Ivy, feeling her eyes brim with tears. 'But I can't wear it. It would be like betraying Jackson.'

Ivy nodded and slipped an arm around her shoulders. 'I know. This is what I've been trying to tell you. Alex needs to understand that you're taken.'

Olivia felt like such a fool! Why hadn't she seen this situation coming? 'This is too much. I've got to tell him about Jackson. Now.'

Chapter Eight

As Olivia hurried away to find Prince Alex, Ivy decided that she'd go and see if her grandmother needed any more help with the party arrangements. She also wanted to ask something about Tessa.

She found the Countess in the ballroom – it wasn't as big as the one at the palace, but it still looked incredible.

Individual black and red candles, not yet lit, hung from the high ceiling with invisible thread to look like they were floating. Tall glass vases filled with deep red rose petals sat on tables covered in rich velvet, and marble statues of Greek gods and goddesses were dotted around the edges of the dance floor. In one corner was a large mahogany dining table.

'What do you think?' the Countess asked as she poured more petals into one of the vases.

'It totally sucks,' Ivy said, and then realised her grandmother might not know the slang. 'That means it's the best.'

The Countess smiled and gave Ivy a quick hug. 'I'm glad to see that you and your sister made up after yesterday.'

'You were right, Grandmother,' Ivy said. 'We did talk it out and nothing like that will ever happen again.'

The Countess sighed. 'It's hard to say that, my dear. You see, when someone you love upsets you, you get even angrier than you would normally, because it hurts that much more.'

The Countess started arranging small name cards with black and red hearts in front of each place setting. 'Your father would always help me with the decorations for the ball. I miss those days.' She sighed and Ivy wanted to give her another hug. The Countess kept talking. 'I miss my son more than anything and wish I could say the right thing to him, so that he would forgive me for turning him away all those years ago.'

The Countess sank down into one of the red velvet chairs. 'Part of me wishes that he had never left Transylvania. But I am so grateful that he did because it means that now we have you and Olivia.' The Countess reached out to hold Ivy's hand. 'Two wonderful granddaughters that I want to keep close to me forever. Families should stay together.'

Ivy gave her grandmother a hug. 'I love that I've been able to meet you and I know Olivia is, too . . . But our home is in Franklin Grove.'

The Countess nodded. 'I know.' She wiped a tear away.

'We'll visit again and you can come to see us,' Ivy offered. 'I'm sure Dad won't mind.'

'Of course, darling,' the Countess said and went back to arranging the name cards. 'Your father will come around eventually. At least he came here with you this time. Who knows what might happen in the future!'

There was a silence and Ivy hoped it was true. She wanted her dad to love her grandparents as much as she did.

Then, Ivy remembered why she had come looking for her grandmother.

'I hope it is OK to ask you this,' Ivy began, and the Countess looked up.

'You can ask me anything, Ivy,' she replied.

'Why don't the servants get to enjoy the

Valentine's Day Ball with everyone else?' Ivy asked, watching her grandmother's face carefully.

'They do, sweetheart,' the Countess replied, looking concerned. 'What do you mean?'

Ivy was relieved that the Countess wasn't dismissive. 'Well, I was talking to Tessa and she said she has to work at the ball. I didn't think that was fair.'

The Countess frowned. 'Hmm. Well, it's true that the staff attend but they are there to serve drinks and keep things moving along.' She paused. 'But maybe we should work it out so that each of them gets some time off during the evening to enjoy the festivities, too.'

'So, you wouldn't mind if Tessa got ready with us?' Ivy asked.

'Of course not, my darling,' her grandmother replied. 'In fact, I think I shall request that all the staff dress for the occasion, rather than wear their uniforms.'

Ivy decided then and there that she was going to find a way for Tessa to show up tonight on an equal footing with Her High and Mighty Majesty. 'Thank you, Grandmother,' she said, giving her a kiss on the cheek. She leaped to her feet, ready to run and tell Olivia the good news.

But what she saw in the doorway froze her like a statue: a blond-haired, blue-eyed, familiar face was holding a big backpack and grinning at her.

'Jackson Caulfield,' Ivy breathed.

'The one and only,' he said, winking. Then he turned to Ivy's grandmother. 'Countess Lazar,' Jackson said, giving a formal bow. 'I'm Jackson Caulfield.' He strode across the room towards the Countess. 'This room looks incredible.'

'Why, thank you,' the Countess said, smiling.

'You must be the friend that my son was talking about.'

Ivy was confused. 'What's going on?'

'Well,' Jackson said, 'I wanted to do something really special for Olivia for Valentine's Day and when I heard that she wasn't even going to be in the country, I had to do something drastic. Mr Vega let me in on the details of your trip here and the ball. I couldn't resist showing up as a surprise. So . . . surprise!'

Ivy gulped. 'Surprise . . .' she replied weakly. All Ivy could think about was Olivia walking into the ball on Alex's arm. *This is spiralling totally out of control*, she thought, gulping hard. *This could not get any worse.*

'Does Olivia like the dress?' Jackson asked, eyes shining.

Oh no. It's just got worse. The dress was from Jackson. Alex hadn't sent it after all . . . which meant that Olivia was about to make a fool of herself!

'Ivy?' Jackson asked, his smile faltering. 'Is everything OK? You look . . . pale.'

'No, no, everything's fine,' she said, rushing to give him a quick welcome hug. 'Absolutely great. Olivia will be thrilled to see you!' She was smiling so hard she thought her face would break.

'You sent a dress?' the Countess asked, clearly impressed.

'She loves it,' Ivy said.

Jackson's mysterious text message, the perfect-for-Olivia dress, even the odd meeting in the mall could be explained by Jackson's Valentine's Day plan.

Ivy realised that S-U-R-P-R-I-S-E really spelled D-I-S-A-S-T-E-R. Olivia was with Prince Alex right now, thinking the dress was from him. She was also thinking that Jackson might not even like her any more. And to top it all off, Olivia had a date for the ball that wasn't her boyfriend.

Ivy was going to have to find her sister before Jackson did and warn her. She decided to get him out of the way first.

'Um, great!' Ivy said brightly. 'Why don't I take you on a tour of the house and show you to your room?'

'He's in the east wing, near your father,' the Countess said.

'East wing,' Ivy muttered.

As long as Olivia and Alex aren't on the way to the east wing, we'll be fine, Ivy thought to herself.

'Why don't we drop off your stuff before we find my sister?' Ivy suggested and didn't wait for a response. She grabbed Jackson's elbow and steered him out of the ballroom and down the hallway. They passed a grandfather clock, ticking loudly. Ivy tried to control the simmering panic. *Time's running out*, she realised. *And I'm the only one who can fix this!*

🦇   🦇   🦇

'This is a beautiful room,' Olivia said, looking up at the floor-to-ceiling shelves of books in the library. 'I haven't had a chance to look at it closely yet.'

Prince Alex gave her a curious look. 'But we sat in here and talked yesterday,' he said.

'Oh, um, that's right.' Alex was thinking of Ivy's impersonation, she realised. 'But a collection like this can always be examined more thoroughly.' She hoped that was enough to cover her slip-up.

She set the box with the dress down between them. 'You've gone out of your way to welcome me to Transylvania, and I'm really grateful.'

'I'm happy to,' Alex said. Olivia tried not to

wince. He really was such a nice guy and having to tell him that she only wanted to be friends made her feel awful.

She was just going to have to come right out and say it. 'I am honoured to walk into the ball on your arm but –'

'But not as honoured as I will be,' Alex interrupted.

Olivia tried again. 'I mean, I know that it's Valentine's Day –'

'The day to spend with the one you love,' Alex cut in.

This could not get any worse, Olivia thought.

She took a deep breath. 'Look, Alex, I just don't feel that way about you.'

Alex sat back a little and blinked.

Olivia rushed on. 'I'm sorry not to have said anything sooner, but I have a boyfriend and –'

His eyebrows furrowed and he tilted his

head to one side. 'I know that.'

'You know?' Olivia was caught off guard.

'Well, I didn't know that you had a boyfriend, but I knew you weren't interested in me,' he replied. 'You didn't think I . . .' Alex began and Olivia realised that he didn't look hurt at all. Just confused.

'Um, well, I . . .' Olivia didn't know what to say now.

'Olivia, I think you are an amazing person – so positive and kind, even when some people disapprove.' Alex smiled at her. 'But I could not be interested in you romantically.' He paused for a breath. 'My heart belongs to someone else.'

Olivia was dumbfounded. 'Who?'

'You haven't guessed?' Alex said with a sad smile on his face. 'I would have thought to someone as romantic as you it would have been obvious.'

'Er . . .' Olivia blinked. 'I haven't noticed.'

But at least it isn't me, she thought, relieved that she wasn't offending him at all.

'What about the dress?' Olivia asked.

'What dress?' Alex responded.

She pointed at the big box on the table. 'That dress.'

'I did not give you a dress,' Alex said.

Now Olivia was completely baffled. 'But if you didn't . . . then who did?'

'Don't you want a moment to rest? A nap, perhaps?' Ivy almost pleaded. She'd delayed Jackson as much as she could on the way up, but couldn't keep it going forever.

He dumped his backpack on the red-patterned carpet and had a quick look around the bedroom. It had a beautiful view over the lake, dozens of old-looking framed maps on the walls and a gold inlay wooden dresser and wardrobe.

'Beautiful,' he said and then turned to leave. Ivy needed more time.

'I came to see Olivia, and I don't want to waste another minute,' he declared.

Ivy sighed. Jackson was going to find Olivia alone with Alex, who was probably spouting poetry to her this very second. *Maybe*, she thought, *if I steer him clear for long enough, she'll be back in our room.*

'OK, let's see if we can find her,' she replied cheerfully. She led him out of the hall and paused for a moment, pretending to be considering which way to go. Then she turned away from the nearest staircase.

'What do you think of this?' Ivy asked, pausing in front of a painting of a flower pot.

'It looks like all those flowers are dead,' Jackson replied.

'Mmm,' Ivy replied, pretending to consider it. 'The artist must have been commenting on the whole genre of still life. What is life when it is still?' She had no idea what she was saying but she hoped it sounded good.

'Yeah, that's deep,' Jackson said, not engaging. 'Can we find Olivia now?'

She stayed in front of the painting for another moment. Jackson looked like he was going to run off on his own. She tried to keep him up on the third floor as long as she could, but he caught on when they passed their second staircase.

'Shouldn't we go downstairs?' Jackson asked.

'Um, yes, but the first two were . . . under construction,' Ivy lied.

'Really?' Jackson didn't look like he believed her but he followed her down one of the middle staircases.

When they made it to the ground floor, they

had a choice, either to walk through the main entrance or to go the long way, past the kitchens. There were people buzzing around everywhere – extra catering staff, people carrying crates of wine glasses. Preparations for the ball were in full swing.

The long way it is, Ivy thought. 'Let's go in this direction!'

But after turning a corner into a second hallway, her super-vamp hearing picked up the sound of Olivia's voice in a room ahead of them – followed by Alex's.

'Um, actually,' Ivy said. 'I've gone the wrong way – let's go back. I think there's a statue back there that I should have pointed out to you.'

Jackson stopped and crossed his arms. 'Ivy, are you hiding something?'

'Uh . . .' Ivy winced. Her Night Stalker skills had deserted her. 'Of course not, I just . . .'

'You took me to see the portraits of the family horses, and then offered a viewing of the incredible feat of raking the gravel on the front drive. I've seen every potted plant in the house and, while fascinating, I know more than I ever wanted to about the history of the Lazar family. Now you want to retrace our steps for a *statue*. I'm no detective – although I have played one – but it seems to me like something funny is going on.'

'No, no!' Ivy wanted to smack her forehead but that would give the game away. The worst thing she could have done was get up his suspicions – well, the worst thing besides leading him straight to Olivia and Alex.

The sound of Olivia laughing floated clearly down the hallway.

'Olivia!' declared Jackson and headed in that direction.

'I–I think that was just the TV,' Ivy stammered, hurrying after him.

'I don't know why you're being so weird,' Jackson said, pausing outside the library door.

'Have you seen the lake?' Ivy tried as a last-ditch effort. 'It's really beautiful –'

But Jackson was already pushing open the door. Wider, wider . . . *Oh no!* Ivy could see Olivia giving Alex a big hug – and so could Jackson.

Olivia's boyfriend stood in the open doorway, watching her embracing someone else.

It doesn't get any worse than this, Ivy thought, peeking from behind her fingers.

Chapter Nine

Olivia turned to the door and gasped. She pulled away from Alex and blurted out the first thing that came into her mind. 'What on earth are you doing here?'

Then she realised that sounded rude. 'I mean, hi, Jackson!'

She'd only been comforting Alex, but she could guess what it must have looked like to Jackson. She hurried over to give him a hug but he seemed stiff and didn't really hug her back.

Olivia looked at Ivy, who offered a sympathetic shrug.

'Surprise,' he said but Olivia could see he was staring at Alex. Staring hard.

'I'm Alex.' The prince reached out to shake Jackson's hand. 'Olivia has just been singing your praises.'

'It's true,' Olivia said. 'I was just saying how much I wished you could be here for Valentine's Day. And here you are!'

'Here I am,' Jackson said with a cold stare. He shook hands with Alex but didn't look happy about it. Olivia had only ever seen him look angry once, and it was in a movie when he'd played an evil robot. 'What's going on, Olivia?'

'I know it looks bad,' Olivia began but Alex stepped in.

'There's been a mix-up,' he said. 'Olivia thought that I was interested in her and was just telling me how she was your girlfriend.'

'So why all the hugging?' Jackson asked Olivia.

'We're just friends,' she said. She could feel her face blushing. 'There's someone else he wants to be with, but he hasn't told me who.'

She looked into Jackson's eyes, hoping that he would understand. *Please don't be mad. We haven't done anything wrong.* She forced herself not to look away, knowing how guilty that would make her look. After a moment, his face softened and a small smile appeared.

'Surprised?' he said.

'Definitely surprised!' Olivia breathed out with relief, and gave him another hug. This time he hugged her back.

Ivy piped up. 'Alex, why don't you and I leave the two lovebirds alone?'

'Very good,' he said, bowing. 'I haven't spent much time with you this visit.' As they walked outside, Olivia heard him say, 'Tell me, Ivy, do you read poetry?'

As the door closed behind them, Jackson sat down on one of the big leather chairs and pulled Olivia on to his lap.

'I've missed you,' Olivia said. 'You should have told me you were coming.'

'That would've kind of ruined the surprise,' Jackson replied, his blue eyes sparkling.

'What about all the publicity for your book?' Olivia asked.

'Nothing like as important as seeing my girlfriend on Valentine's Day,' he said and Olivia felt her heart thumping faster.

'It didn't seem that important when I saw you at the book signing.' Olivia remembered how miserable she had felt when he'd walked away to that VIP party.

'I know. I'm sorry,' he said. 'When I'm working, I'm always pulled in a hundred directions.' He grinned. 'The trouble was that I knew I was coming here and so I had in the back of my mind that it wouldn't matter because I'd be seeing you soon. Didn't you get my text message?'

Olivia poked him in the side. 'Yes, but that didn't help! I didn't know what it meant.'

He grinned. 'Well, I'm full of Valentine's Day surprises. First, there was the dress . . .'

'Which is so perfect,' Olivia said.

'And . . .'

'And . . .?' Olivia sat up.

'And there's an even bigger one.' He looked like he'd just won an Academy Award.

'I don't see how it's possible to be bigger than showing up out of the blue in a whole different country and choosing the most exquisite dress I've ever seen,' Olivia countered.

'Ah, well,' he said. 'If it's not possible, I'd better call the whole thing off, then.'

Olivia poked him again. 'Tell me!'

He gave her a big hug. 'My parents are viewing houses in Franklin Grove as we speak. All three of us are tired of the crazy Hollywood scene, and they agreed that Franklin Grove is a beautiful place to settle.'

Olivia gasped. 'What?'

'I want to go to a regular school, have regular classes.' Jackson looked into her eyes. 'I want to be near you.'

Olivia felt like she was floating somewhere near the ceiling. 'You're moving?'

'And I've told Amy that I'll be doing fewer events and more studying.'

Jackson beamed and Olivia beamed back.

'Oh my goodness,' Olivia said. She jumped up and did a little happy dance. 'You are the BEST!'

'I was hoping you'd say that,' Jackson said.

Olivia closed her eyes. Things couldn't have turned out more perfectly. Not only did Jackson go all out for Valentine's Day, he was moving his whole life just to be near her!

'Why is your dress in the library?' Jackson asked.

Olivia grabbed the box on the table and clutched it to her. 'Because I thought Alex had given it to me and I couldn't accept it. But now that I know it was you I am never letting it go!'

'Good,' Jackson said. 'You'll be the most beautiful girl at the ball tonight.'

Olivia nodded, but then it hit her. She had agreed to go with Prince Alex.

Eek!

'Actually, Jackson, there's something I need to . . .'

But Jackson grabbed her in another hug and she didn't want to spoil the moment.

It can wait, Olivia thought.

Tessa held the mirror up behind Ivy's head so that she could see the spiked fan of hair that she'd styled to splay out from her bun.

'It's fantastic,' Ivy said. 'Thank you.'

'It's my pleasure,' Tessa replied. 'You look stunning. Do you want to see the whole thing together?'

Ivy stepped in front of the full-length mirror. The dress Georgia had loaned her was a strapless black silk bodice with a full skirt. The toes of the Victorian lace-up heeled boots poked out from under the hem. With her heavy black eyeliner, Ivy looked like a fashion goth.

'The dress is gorgeous,' Ivy said, pulling up the bodice. 'But I just don't look like me.'

She wished she could throw on one of her own skirts and feel *comfortable*. It's what she'd wanted ever since she'd arrived in Transylvania.

Just then, the computer on her desk pinged

with a new email. Tessa helped her with the cumbersome skirt over to the chair.

The subject heading was BE MY VALEN-TINE and the email just had a link and the words, 'Love, Brendan.'

'Who's Brendan?' Tessa asked as Ivy clicked on the link.

'He's my boyfriend,' Ivy replied, smiling in anticipation of what he'd sent her.

The link went straight to a video clip.

'Hi, Ivy!' said Brendan on-screen, pushing his hair out of his face. He leaned in closer. 'Is it on?' he asked himself and then sat back. 'Yup, it's on. OK. This is my Valentine's video for you, because I wish you were here and I love you.' He smiled and the image clicked over to a big picture of the Franklin Grove gang outside the Meat and Greet: Ivy, Brendan, Olivia, Sophia and Camilla. A song started. Ivy knew it right away: 'Stalk You

Tonight' by the Dark Violets.

Photos flashed on the screen: Ivy and Brendan playing air hockey, Ivy and Brendan's sister Bethany playing with Bethany's gothified Barbies, Ivy and Sophia having a black pen fight in which Sophia drew a big bunny on Ivy's bicep.

Ivy hugged herself as the video went on, making her feel happy and homesick at the same time. At the end, there were three photos in a row: Brendan standing in his backyard making an 'I' by standing up with his arms above his head, making a heart with his arms over his head and then pointing at the screen with a huge grin.

'I love you, too,' Ivy whispered, stroking the necklace at her throat.

'He seems like an awesome boyfriend,' Tessa said, giving a deep sigh.

Ivy nodded. *The necklace was a nice Valentine's Day present*, she thought. *But that was perfection.*

'Tell me about Jackson,' Tessa said. 'He must be a pretty amazing boyfriend, too, to fly all the way out here to surprise Olivia.'

Ivy nodded. 'They are totally meant to be together, although Olivia was a little worried that he'd forgotten Valentine's Day altogether. I'm glad he's here to work everything out – and I'm glad the whole Alex and Olivia thing is out of the way. I mean, he's a prince!'

Tessa winced. 'Yes, I suppose a prince and a normal girl is a silly idea.'

The tone in her voice made Ivy's spy senses perk up. Slowly, a pattern began to form in her head. She remembered Alex glaring after his mother was rude to Tessa over the tea, and how wistful he was talking about playing with Tessa on the fountain when he broke his arm.

Olivia had said: *someone else he wants to be with*. Ivy thought of all the times she'd seen Tessa upset and all the tension between her and the Queen. When Alex skated away on the lake, it could have been because he couldn't face her – because he was hurting.

'It's you!' Ivy declared. '*You're* the "someone else" Alex wants.'

Tears filled Tessa's eyes. 'It's true. We're in love. We grew up together and had always been really good friends. Then, last summer we went horseback riding together in the woods.' Tessa smiled through her tears. 'We stopped for a picnic in a field of daisies and he kissed me. It was the most romantic, wonderful moment of my life.' She sniffled. 'But his mother has forbidden us to be together.'

'That's awful,' Ivy said, putting her arm around Tessa.

'She's dead against us because my family were servants.' Tessa's eyes flashed. 'She'd rather make her son miserable than allow a commoner like me into her family. It would almost be better if I were a human.'

Ivy sat down on her coffin with a thump. All the time she had thought Alex was being mean to Tessa, but he was really just in pain.

'This isn't fair,' Ivy said. 'His mother is trying to force you both into being someone that you're not.'

'I'd like to talk to her,' Tessa said, 'but she refuses to give me an audience. I just want her to see who I am . . . to see behind my uniform.'

An idea started to form in Ivy's mind. One that might actually work.

'I've a plan,' Ivy declared, 'and you are not allowed to say no.'

Chapter Ten

Outside the ballroom, Olivia was wringing her gloved hands together and pacing up and down — hard to do in a floor-length silk dress.

There was a buzz of noise from inside the ballroom, soft music and people chattering. Olivia wanted to know who was in there and what the room looked like. Ivy had said the decorations were killer.

More than that, she wanted to be *inside* so that she could avoid the whole walking-in-with-Alex issue. But, being part of the host's family, her arrival had to be announced. She had strict instructions from the Countess to wait by this third entrance door once most of the guests had arrived.

The trouble was that she still hadn't told Jackson about being presented with Alex.

I should have said something! Olivia scolded herself. But their moment in the library had been so delicate and so happy that she hadn't wanted to mess it up.

She turned on the spot, ready to march across the hallway again and almost tripped on her hem, Ivy-style.

Get a grip! Olivia told herself.

She heard footsteps and looked up to see Jackson striding towards her. She had never seen him looking so handsome. He was wearing a tailored tux with satin lapels and shiny shoes. He had a handkerchief in his pocket the exact colour of her dress.

Jackson bent at the hips and kissed her hand. 'Mademoiselle,' he said, seeming to enjoy the formality, 'you look stunning.'

Olivia felt her heart leap. This was such a special moment, but she was going to have to tell him right away. Any minute, everyone else would arrive.

She took a breath. 'Jackson, I don't want you to think anything of this . . .'

'You mean, of this wonderfully romantic Valentine's Day ball?' Jackson asked, grinning.

'Um,' Olivia said. *Being so sweet about this is only making it worse!* she thought. 'It's not necessarily romantic,' she protested.

Jackson started to dance with her, smoothly. She could smell musky cologne and wanted to just melt into his arms.

'I think it is,' he whispered.

Olivia closed her eyes. She had to tell him.

'Jackson, before you arrived, I agreed with Alex that I –'

'You two are such a great couple,' came a voice from behind Jackson. It was Prince Alex, looking very smart with his hair slicked back, and wearing a white tuxedo.

Jackson pulled away from her and turned to face him. 'Thank you.'

Olivia felt the panic rising up. This was the moment – Jackson was going to be stunned and probably super mad. He'd made so much effort to make her Valentine's Day special and she'd ruined it.

Alex gave Olivia a wink. 'You're going to be the envy of the ball, walking in together.'

Olivia's knees went weak. 'Really? Thank you,' she said, hoping he knew she meant for being so understanding.

Prince Alex turned to Jackson. 'I hear from

Ivy that you play a mean game of tennis?'

Jackson smiled. 'I try.'

'We'll have to see how you do tomorrow, then,' Alex said. 'The courts at the palace are covered, so we can play year round.'

'You're on!' Jackson said with a smile.

Olivia wondered what Alex was going to do about walking in with someone. 'What about you . . .' she began.

'Don't worry,' Alex said. 'Ivy sent word with Nadia that she'd rescue me.'

'Your Highness,' Olivia said with a curtsy. 'You have been so nice, the whole trip. I'm very glad I got to meet you.'

'That's what friends are for,' he replied.

The Countess clicked down the hallway towards them in a purple sparkling dress, incredible dangling diamond earrings and silver high heels. 'Oh, good, you're here! We're just about to be announced. Everyone's waiting.'

The Count followed behind, looking dashing in a grey morning suit with a deep red cravat. His moustache looked bushier than Ivy had ever seen it.

'Have you . . .' the Countess asked quietly. 'Is your father feeling better? And where's Ivy?'

Olivia bit her lip and shook her head. 'I haven't seen him since this afternoon. Ivy, er, she says she'll catch us up.' Whatever Ivy's plan was, she hoped the Countess wouldn't ask any more questions. *I don't know how long I can cover for her!*

'No matter,' the Countess said. 'You'll escort me, won't you, my husband?'

'I would be delighted, my darling wife.' They gave each other a quick kiss.

Olivia knew it would mean so much to her grandmother if her son would walk her into the ball, but at least she and the Count made such a cute old couple. She took Jackson's hand and hoped they would end up like that.

'The tradition is that Her Majesty enters first,' the Countess said, looking back down the hallway.

As if on cue, the Queen turned the corner with two attendants carrying her impressive train. Her dress was deep red satin with sparkling beads intricately woven into heart-shaped patterns. Olivia thought she looked like a pretty version of the Queen of Hearts.

Everyone curtsied and bowed.

'Dear Caterina,' said the Queen graciously. 'I am so looking forward to this evening. Happy Valentine's Day. Thank you for hosting and for all that you do for me as a friend.'

'Happy Valentine's Day,' the Countess replied. 'You are most welcome.'

The Queen gave Alex a quick kiss on the

cheek and stepped in front of the double doors just as they opened.

Olivia looked around for her sister, wondering why she hadn't appeared yet. *Does this have something to do with Ivy 'rescuing' Alex?* she thought.

'What a shame Ivy's still not here,' the Countess said, looking around.

'Too late!' whispered the Count.

'Ladies and gentlemen,' boomed Horatio to the crowd that filled the ballroom.

Olivia was amazed by the dresses and the decorations. Over a hundred faces were watching the door in anticipation.

'May I present Her Majesty, Queen Stephanie of Transylvania!' said Horatio.

Everyone inside curtsied and bowed as the Queen strode in. She made her way around the crowd, wishing them all a Happy Valentine's Day.

'Shall we?' said the Count to the Countess.

'Wait!' a voice called from down the hallway and Olivia glanced back, almost clapping with delight when she saw her bio-dad hurrying down the hall, looking suave in his black tuxedo with a black shirt underneath.

'Wait,' Charles said again, his face flushed. 'I would . . .' He paused and smiled awkwardly. 'I would like to escort you in, Mother. If you would have me.'

He held out the crook of his arm and Olivia saw tears of happiness in her grandmother's eyes. 'Of course, my son. Of course.'

'I shouldn't have been so churlish,' he admitted. 'You've been nothing but welcoming to my family since we've arrived and I think it's time for . . . for some harmony.'

In the doorway, Horatio's eyes glistened. Olivia felt a bit tearful herself and couldn't stop smiling.

I'm so proud of you, she thought, beaming at her father.

The Count proudly stepped aside so that the Countess could link her arm through her son's. Together, they stepped into the doorway.

Olivia heard murmurings of surprise coming from inside the ballroom.

Horatio smiled as he called out, 'The Countess Caterina Lazar and her son, the Viscount Charles Vega.'

They stepped in unison into the room and began to greet guests.

Horatio leaned over and whispered to Olivia, 'This is my favourite Valentine's Ball ever.'

Olivia beamed. 'Mine, too.' She turned to Jackson. 'It's us next, I think!'

He gave her a huge hug and then took her hand. 'You're the only girl for me, Olivia,' he said and Olivia's heart burst into happy confetti.

Horatio smiled at Olivia and said, 'Miss Olivia Abbott and Mr Jackson Caulfield.'

Olivia felt like she was stepping on to the field in front of crammed bleachers, except for all the ball gowns. She smiled so wide her cheeks ached.

She glanced behind her quickly to see Prince Alex waiting in the hall with the Count. There was still no sign of Ivy. *Where is she?* Olivia thought.

Then, the Countess was introducing her and Jackson to the Mayor of Bucharest, who wore a dark tailored suit with a colourful sash across his chest. His wife was wearing a beautiful cream gown and sparkling tiara.

Next in line, Olivia was surprised to see Nadia, wearing a pretty floral dress and her hair all in curls. 'Tessa did my hair,' she whispered, her eyes shining. 'And it's all because of Ivy that I got to dress up!'

'When did you last see Ivy?' Olivia wanted

to know, but Nadia was already speaking to the Countess.

'You do look lovely, dear,' said the Countess.

Nadia curtsied and then nearly fainted when Jackson reached out to shake her hand.

Just then, Olivia heard Horatio say, 'The Count Nicholas Lazar and his granddaughter Miss Ivy Vega!'

Ivy walked into the ballroom, feeling like she could take on the world. She was wearing her own fitted black dress with horizontal zipper decorations and a little paper red heart dangling from the zipper near her right shoulder. Best of all, she was wearing her clompy boots.

She felt comfortable, happy and little bit wicked.

'I thought you were going to wear Georgia's dress,' Olivia said as Ivy and the Count approached.

'I was,' Ivy said simply.

'And what about Prince Alex?' Olivia wanted to know. Her face wore a mixture of awe, pride and nerves.

'You'll see,' Ivy replied. She could barely contain her glee.

The crowd gasped collectively. One woman lifted her black lace fan over her face and another leaned over to whisper in her friend's ruby-adorned ear.

Ivy already knew what they were seeing. She turned to watch Prince Alex and Tessa smiling at each other, standing in the doorway side by side, holding hands.

Horatio said, loudly and clearly, 'His Highness Prince Alexander of Transylvania and . . . Miss Tessa Lupescu.'

Tessa looked incredible in Georgia's dress. Instead of a braid, her long hair was tumbling over her shoulders. She was a couple of inches taller than Ivy and looked as stunning as any catwalk model. And in the high-heeled Victorian boots, she walked with the confidence of a model, too.

Prince Alex didn't say anything, but he didn't need to. It was obvious to all these high-society vampires that these two people were in love.

'I thought I was the one who did the matchmaking,' Olivia whispered, giving her sister a nudge. 'Well done.'

Ivy looked over to the Queen. She looked stunned, one gloved hand on her heart. But as the happy couple began greeting guests, her face softened.

It was clear to everyone that they seemed to fit together so well. Tessa laughed nervously and Alex kept one hand firmly on her waist.

'I just hope that the Queen might start to

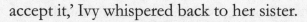

accept it,' Ivy whispered back to her sister.

The band struck up the first song and couples moved on to the dance floor.

'My beautiful daughters.' Mr Vega appeared in front of them. 'I must say thank you for bringing me here, for showing me what family is all about.' He bowed formally. 'If I could, I would dance with you both.'

'Luckily –' Jackson stepped over – 'I can help with that. Olivia?' He bowed and held out his hand which Olivia accepted.

Ivy chuckled as her father did the same for her.

While Olivia's cheerleader training helped her pick up the steps very easily, and Jackson's movie training came in handy for him, Ivy and Charles lingered near the edge, giggling as they pretended to dance.

Prince Alex and Tessa waltzed past in sync. To

Ivy Tessa looked just like a princess should.

'Thank you,' Tessa mouthed as they floated past.

'Not quite our scene, is it, Ivy?' said Mr Vega as they waddled back and forth.

'But I'm having fun,' Ivy admitted.

Just then, the Queen walked up to them. 'I believe you are responsible for my son's happiness this evening.'

Ivy blinked and stopped dancing. *Did that mean she's not going to have my head chopped off?*

'The Lazar family has a way of changing things,' the Queen said.

'What do you mean, Your Majesty?' Mr Vega said.

'First,' she said, 'your parents have been pestering me for years about being more inclusive with humans and, secondly, your daughter has shown me that I should also

242

trust my son's judgement more than I have.' She glanced across the dance floor at Alex and Tessa, then looked pointedly at Mr Vega. 'Times do change, sir.'

She swished away, her train trailing across the wooden floor.

Ivy's dad looked stunned, but he smiled. 'That was a surprise,' he said to Ivy, taking up her hands again and starting to dance.

Just then, the Countess clapped her hands. 'Ladies and gentlemen,' she called. 'Thank you very much for attending. We are so happy to have our family together on Valentine's Day, knowing that there is so much love under our roof. We hope that you share those loving feelings and that you enjoy this song, chosen especially for my wonderful granddaughters.'

She signalled to the band. After the first few notes, Ivy recognised the song. It was 'Together

Eternally' by The Killer Bees, one of her favourite bands.

Olivia hurried over with Jackson, Alex and Tessa. The Count and Countess came too, and the eight of them formed a circle, with the younger generation shouting out the words to the song.

For the first time since she'd arrived, Ivy felt like she truly belonged.

TWIN TALK!

In this new interview, VAMP magazine's Georgia Huntingdon talks to the two most unlikely twins in the world about a visit to their ancestral homeland, and what it was like hanging out in Vampire High Society.

Georgia Huntingdon: So, Ivy, you got to visit Transylvania — the home of vampires — on Valentine's Day. Tell us about that.

Ivy Vega: High-society vamps are even sappier about Valentine's Day than the bunniest of bunnies. [Laughs] Seriously — they go all out. I think even Olivia thought it was a bit much!

Georgia: For an ordinary American girl like you —

Ivy: [interrupting] I don't think anyone's ever called me 'ordinary' before.

Georgia: Well, you know what I mean. For a girl who has grown up in a quiet, normal-ish American town, being around such . . . *posh* vampires must have been something of a culture shock.

Ivy: Oh yes, definitely. I have never in my life seen so many knives and forks at a dinner table — I probably could have made a large robot out of them! I honestly thought most of them were just spares, in case any of the guests dropped their cutlery. Not that that was likely to happen — rich vamps aren't exactly messy.

Georgia: Has discovering your aristocratic background affected your normal life in Franklin Grove in anyway?

Ivy: Not really, because only my vamp friends know the truth – and they would sooner take a garlic bath than bow and scrape before me! While I was there, I saw a lot of servant vamps all standing quietly and formally before the Queen and Prince Alex – it was very strange. I don't think I'd like to have anyone doing that in front of me. There were servants at my grandparents' house who were all 'Miss Ivy' this and 'Miss Olivia' that – it made me a little uncomfortable.

Georgia: I can imagine that you and protocol don't quite match up.

Ivy: Certainly not.

Georgia: It sounds like you didn't have the best of times.

Ivy: Oh no, no, no – I don't mean to sound like I hated Transylvania. I liked it a lot. It was really cool to be there, to finally meet my grandparents, and to see where my dad grew up. Plus, if I did hate it, I wouldn't have even considered going back.

Georgia: That's right, your life path did take you back to Transylvania. But we're going to get to that in a later interview. Before we change subjects, one last thing on Transylvania . . . Did it feel like it could be home?

Ivy: I . . . I don't understand.

Georgia: Well, your family is part of the royal bloodline. Your grandparents are the Count and Countess, which means . . .

Ivy: Oh . . . yes, right . . . One day, I will be Countess Ivy. Oh my darkness, that sounds so weird to say!

Georgia: Do you think you will be ready, when the time comes?

Ivy: [long pause] That is a long way off. Like, decades. I don't want to worry about that yet.

Georgia: So, Olivia – since it's now OK for us to talk openly about your love life, I'm going to start bugging you!

Olivia Abbott: Uh oh. [Laughs]

Georgia: What's the hardest part of dating a movie star?

Olivia: I suppose it's the time spent apart. Jackson's work is not just about acting – there's all sorts of other stuff that eats up his time – interviews and personal appearances.

Georgia: Like when he came to the Franklin Grove mall to sign copies of his book?

Olivia: Yes, exactly. Who knew spending a day at the mall could be such hard work?

Georgia: What was it like to see that hundreds and hundreds of other girls had packed out the local mall to get a glimpse of *your* boyfriend?

Olivia: Quite strange, I'm not going to lie. I knew that I should have been feeling smug, because I was his real-life girlfriend, but I didn't. To be honest, I felt . . . frustrated, because I knew that our relationship was not going to be normal. It might never be normal, ever. And Jackson doesn't even know my family's secret!

Georgia: But so much other stuff in your life is hardly 'normal' – maybe you and a movie star are a perfect match?

Olivia: [smiles] Maybe. I never thought of it like that. My life can sometimes be as wacky as a movie star's. Although I don't have as many people scrambling for my attention as Jackson does.

Georgia: But if your acting career takes off, maybe you will.

Olivia: Hmm . . . I'm not sure I'd like that. I think Jackson handles the attention really well – he's always so polite, even though he must be tired and annoyed deep down. But he never shows it.

Georgia: You're hardly a stranger to attention. When you and your sister visited Transylvania, you ended up drawing some admiration – from a real, live Prince!

Olivia: I was hoping this wouldn't be made public. Prince Alex showed an interest in me when I first got to Transylvania, but it was, well . . . complicated. He was just rebelling against his mom, and acting a little crazy because he wasn't allowed to be with the girl he really wanted to be with.

Georgia: Alex was using you? That's not very nice.

Olivia: Alex is a great guy, really. He was just mixed up at the time. People do crazy things when they're in love – believe me, I know. And he and Tessa are just *made* for each other. Her Majesty the Queen changed her mind about whether they could be together, so it all worked out in the end.

Georgia: If Alex had been for real, would you have gone out with him?

Olivia: I don't think so. For the same reason that I don't think I would have gone out with Jackson if he'd been a vamp – it's probably not a good idea.

Georgia: Speaking of Jackson, I heard he made a surprise appearance in Transylvania. And there's that blushing again!

Olivia: Stop it!

Georgia: How romantic was the moment? On a scale of one to 'oh wow!'

Olivia: What comes after 'oh wow'? I was *extremely* happy when Jackson showed up in Transylvania, especially as I'd been a bit worried that he'd become distant with me. I was thrilled that we were back on track. But we hadn't even kissed at that point.

Georgia: But he's a *movie star!*

Olivia: I know. But we were both quite shy!

Georgia: Oh my darkness, I want to shake both of you!

Olivia: Don't worry – we're getting to the kiss. And *that* is a great story . . .

In the next of VAMP magazine's exclusive interviews, the twins tell Georgia about reconnecting with the non-vampire side of their family, and we get all the gossip on Olivia's relationship with Jackson!

Discover the fangtastic new series from Sienna Mercer... These twins will have you howling with laughter!

To their classmates, Daniel and Justin are identical twin brothers. But in fact they couldn't be more different.

On their thirteenth birthday, one of them is destined to turn into a werewolf... This full moon is going to change everything!